For the
Travelling Mind

This is an IndieMosh book

brought to you by MoshPit Publishing
an imprint of Mosher's Business Support Pty Ltd

PO Box 4363
Penrith NSW 2750

indiemosh.com.au

A catalogue record for this
work is available from the
National Library of Australia

https://www.nla.gov.au/collections

Title: For the Travelling Mind

Subtitle: Short Stories, Poems and Thoughts

Author: McIntyre, Benjamin (1991–)

ISBNs: 9781922912503 (paperback)
                9781922912510 (ebook – epub)
                9781922912527 (ebook – Kindle)

Subjects: FICTION: Fantasy/general; Science Fiction/general

1st Edit by Colette Appert

Cover concept and images by Benjamin McIntyre

Cover layout by Sarah Davies at https://lemondesignstudio.com.au/

For the Travelling Mind

Short Stories, Poems and Thoughts

Benjamin McIntyre

I am grateful that I saw this project through, so that I could dedicate it to my favourite author, Sir Terry Pratchett. May his work forever amuse, inspire and enthral all who encounter it.

Book One of
The Adventuring Minds
Series

Contents

Opening Words 1

A Cursed Ending 4

Death's Hall 25

Chased by Demons 29

Hearts Apart 38

A Nurse's Reflection 41

Scent of a New World 51

A Respectful Conversation 57

Tales of the Ogre and the Wolf 62

Love's Journey 70

Riddle Me Your Dreams 75

The Ogre, the Wolf and the Owl 81

Tides of the New Age 100

Jetpacks 103

The lost 214

Closing Words 217

Opening Words

Fiction and history blends
As works from past and present
Come together to flow and crash
From my mind to yours

Expression and imagination
Reason and nonsense
Guide my blind fingers
On a keyboard
Made for our possibly lucky souls

I am a discovery writer
Taking myself on a journey
As words tumble to the page
So that I may share with you
All of you
A part of me

"Light thinks it travels faster than anything, but it is wrong. No matter how fast light travels, it finds the darkness has always got there first, and is waiting for it."

Terry Pratchett, 'Reaper Man'

What is amazing about the human brain, is its ability to fill in gaps of information, drawing on experience and knowledge to expand into the world of imagination.

So really, the words I write on this page, become a vessel for your own brilliance.

A Cursed Ending

Lightning lights up the shadows of the towering mountains all around you, the accompanying thunder crashing into the dark distance. The wind howls its eternal curse, cutting through crevices and ravines, ragged rock faces and the few small trees that manage to survive in this dead, desolate and damned landscape.

The wind tugs at you, as you pull out a small worn note from your thick, woollen coat pocket. Gripping it for dear life in your numb fingers, you reread the neat and curly cursive in the fading light. No longer actually needing it for direction, you hold it more for validation that you might have some sanity left. That this isn't a dream.

> *Follow our star into the mountains from the place of my fall. I have much to discuss with you.*
>
> *A*

You shake your head in disbelief. After all this time, could your old friend actually be alive? That they even managed to get a note to you from such a faraway place is amazing in itself.

Oh, how things have changed over the years. You know that you are different to the person you once were. But perhaps there are some things that haven't changed so much. These things are hard to judge, when yours is the only perspective you have on the circumstance.

You pause, realising that the track you walk on has now become but a small ledge. To your left rises the steep slope of the mountain. On your right, it drops away to what would be your deathly demise. You would cascade over broken rocks and boulders to the bottom, where a river rages below in a small ravine. You know these waters. You know the water will kill you, and not just from the cold. The river has its own life and soul; all devouring and unforgiving. Cracked words come out from between your dry, cracked lips.

"The only change is ... I became more the fool."

Moments pass and you look up to see the Conqueror's Star is becoming obscured by the evening's clouds. You continue through the cutting wind, chasing just a faint sent of smoke. Your backpack is heavy, cutting into your shoulders after walking for several days up through the Cursed Pass, and the last half-day walking the Killer's Path. Whoever named the tracks could not think of more appropriate names. The Windy Arse Pass and Over-blowy track are just as equally appropriate.

Fatigue sets into your bones, and you realise that it is not just physical exhaustion that's getting to you. You have delayed thinking about what you will have to face. Ahead there is a difficult decision for you to make and it will weigh heavy on your soul.

The breeze teases you again with the hint of wood fire smoke, this time stronger than the last. You try not to get your hopes up that your destination could be so close; no one could possibly live out here. However, the hint of smoke lingers this time.

Half an hour later, you nearly miss a hidden track that faintly cuts left into the mountain. You will have to climb it morethan walk it. Suddenly, your mind reels in disbelief as you take in where you are and the turn of events. Wishing things weren't the way they are, your heart pounds in your chest and a wave of anxiety washes over you. You take a deep breath. Even if the track does not lead to where you have been summoned, it might provide shelter for the night. You start the climb.

You slip and catch yourself on the rocks, adrenaline surging at the thought of dying in the freezing waters below. You steel yourself and continue, hands and knees now sore from catching yourself on the cold hard rock.

Minutes later, huffing and puffing, you come to the crest of the path and find yourself looking down into what feels to be the soul of the mountain. It is a deep, wide crevice with a small cave opening in one side. The opening shows silhouetted shadows shimmering around an amber glow that emanates from the ragged opening. The smoke smells so strongly of smouldering cinders that you cannot help but cough.

The shimmering shadows seem to still at the sound, pausing in their dance before they melt into the walls again to resume a more natural flickering. You breathe deeply to steady yourself after your mild coughing fit, and then freeze as an unspoken voice of great depth and age reaches your ears.

"The time is now my friend. Be not afraid. Let us speak as we used to."

With a slow purposeful stride, you move into the cave entrance, grim determination set. You progress further inside, only seeing the walls and curves that make up the bones of the mountain. The shadows and light cast on the rocky surface are not from a flame, but from a fire's soul. There is a Fire Spirit being held here.

You enter a chamber. It is magnificent. All the furnishings are exquisite, appearing to be suspended in time, still new from an age ago. The lush red carpet exudes warmth into the soles of your feet. The bed, the bath, the bookcases, and desk radiate warmth into your heart through their lavish woods, exotic metals, and delicate designs. It is the place that Kings dream, Queens envy, and Empires fall at their knees to make a reality. And it feels like Hell.

Two humble wooden chairs facing each other dominate the centre of the chamber. Seated on one is a figure robed in rich dark silks and simple sandals. The empty chair beside them feels presumptuous in its expectancy, as if they thought this reunion would be as simple as sitting down to talk. The figure stands and the hood falls back to reveal a shaven head of grey flesh, empty eye sockets and only half a jaw, tongue writhing as it tastes the exposed air.

You stare in disbelief at this animated rotting corpse. In a slow controlled manner, you place your bag onto the ground beside you. You know them, this ... thing to be the sender of the note in your pocket but cannot understand how the two could be the same. What happened to your long lost, dear old friend?

While you are still strong and relatively young of body, your friend appears to have aged, a millennium. But that is not what concerns you, as you feel their overwhelming presence. It has not been their body they have been keeping alive all this time. Instead, their spirit has been fed as their physical body wasted away. Their mouth is still but, their tongue continues to writhe out of sync with their unspoken words.

"You look well my old friend. How are you and the family?"

Such a mundane thing to ask. Still, pausing to clear your throat, your thoughts clash and conflict within your mind, making it difficult to consider what to say. As always, respect takes precedence and you let the genuine joy of memories guide your words.

"Thank you. Like me, they are living a happy, carefree life. It was a pleasant surprise to discover you still live old friend."

The half-mouth grins gruesomely, tongue lolling as they bow their head slowly acknowledging your words.

"A surprise it indeed must have been. As much as it was a surprise for me when I discovered you had removed yourself from your contented and joy-filled life to answer my call. Travelling all this way to see someone who you believed to be dead."

You bow your head in solemn response, while your memories cascade on top of each other, a montage of scenes and feelings from glorious battles and horrendous triumphs. Smiling in nostalgia, you focus on the pressure of the present, embracing the presence of your once long-lost friend in front of you. However, you do not move forward to embrace them, but instead keep your distance.

"I have many reasons to see you. Besides simply wanting to see you once again. Curiosity has consumed me the moment I received your note. I can only guess that the forbidden magics finally worked for you ..."

Their grey, leathery claw-like hands come together in front of their chest, head slowly nodding. Words come to your ears, but their mouth does not stir.

"Your guess is correct, however, as you can see it has come at a price. My body has withered in my attempt to stay alive, and the past years, which have felt like an eternity, have been a new battle. A challenge to overcome. But now, I am stronger in mind than I ever was in body before. Perhaps more than yourself. Tell me, do you still hold true to our visions of the world of before, when we tried to make the world anew?"

Your words are the stillness of a frozen lake, but your mind, the turmoil of the river that sits at the bottom of the mountain. As you speak, your mind becomes the tranquillity of your words.

"I feel you know the answer to that already. There was no way that the world could have continued the way it was after you helped shape and mould the future for us. Our efforts and sacrifices saved it from the brutality and waste that was eating away the world. And now that order has been restored to the land, peaceful governance has guided us all into the new era. It exists true to your vision, better than either of us ever imagined or could have hoped for. Slavery is gone, and people live in an empire that values kindness, not blind brutal devotion. I am so grateful that I can say thank you dear friend, for your sacrifices in making it so."

A hiss stings your ears, and their face turns to a snarl. The room becomes heavy and foreboding. The shimmering shadows on the walls ooze onto the bare rocks of the cave floor. However, underlying their harsh reaction, you sense conflicting feelings of endearment and pride from your friend. Perhaps your words are still flattering. You listen closely without interrupting, so as to show respect.

"My dear friend, as much as you are correct, you are also wrong. You're governing a world that is still languishing in pain and torment. Our vision was to rule this age! Rule it so that they, the people, could know the true meaning of peace by removing evil that comes of having to make their own choice.

With our might we were meant to carry their sins for them, as we lived and breathed for them. Is this why you left me behind to die at our enemy's hands? Because you knew that you couldn't do what was needed, even with your power?"

Silence stretches briefly. You hold your tongue knowing you are both gathering your thoughts. Their words continue.

"The truth is ... I was martyred so that you could continue to live with the glory of victory over our predecessors. You killed those closest to us, to our vision, to hide your failures of doing what was needed. Please, tell me how things are better than they were before. Prove me wrong, that you are not blinded by your weakness, or even your over-inflated sense of greatness."

Surely lies! But why do they ring with unpleasant truth. Joyful memories become a twisted façade. For a brief moment, reality is revealed to you. Long forgotten memories of horrors committed against your enemies, and even friends, start reaching and clamouring at the surface of your mind. Things all done in the name of peace. The suppressed memories are no longer contained. Must peace always come at such costs? You gather your resolve by taking a deep breath, calming the waters of your mind and soul. It was never about me. It was for the greater good.

"My friend, you had already saved the world when you exposed our predecessors, our enslavers, to everyone and gave our people the means to overcome them. We showed them how to live. Not as our oppressors had made us in their image but in our own. You shaped that. You guided us all into the new age as we know it. It was misfortune that in the last battle, the battle that you lead, you were left for dead. We searched the battlefield for days, toiling through the dead but to no avail. You had vanished and we had to keep moving. We mourned you, friend, and you were made a hero and an idol for your triumphs. You are considered a god amongst the people, as an everlasting example of all that is good in the world. Even though we know there is more to the story than we could ever tell."

Again, upon hearing your words, you feel their mind project sensations, this time of pride and victory into the room. It lasts for a brief moment before you feel dread replace it. Their hands rise up to cradle their face. No tears appear, but the sorrow and pain weighs so heavily in the air, so strong, that the fire dulls, and everything around you slowly blackens and rots.

"Your words are twisted truths! The fact that you govern instead of rule, tells me that you did not truly hold to my vision and dreams, the goals that we once shared. A better world? Maybe without our predecessors and enslavers, but the same problems remain. Now, will you stand aside as I make things right, again aiding me in assuming the mantle of supreme ruler?"

You stand there, conflicting emotions and thoughts falling away as your decision becomes apparent. Air fills your lungs as you take a long slow breath. No words are spoken by you as you both maintain eye contact.

"Very well. I will re-join the world once again, as a god reborn, to put the people back on the path of what is just and right for them. Try to sway me in this and you will fail. You are not the ruler I had envisioned for this world, lacking the strength to do what is necessary, what needs to be done. I have sat here for too long gathering my strength ... still, it might not be in vain. Leave me my old friend. Do not resist my return and I will leave you in peace. I will be sure to see it all through to the end, unlike you, who left me behind."

Thunder cracks outside, punctuating your old friend's words. You do not jump, however, the electricity in the air leaves you feeling charged and ready. This is not how you wanted it to happen, but you knew; you knew that this was a possibility the moment you held their note in your hand. You also knew that too much had changed over the years for you to welcome back your old friend. The world no longer reflects the old ideas of a ruler long gone.

Your voice, when it sounds, does not belong to the you of now, but to the you of old. You, who paid so much in blood for what you believed in. You, who broke and reshaped the world physically and metaphysically. Your voice, equal to that of the revered individual in front of you, now carries the weight of the new world. Your home. Your family.

"No."

Silence. You both stare at each other. The world holds its breath. Nothing needs to be said. All has been communicated in every sense possible and you both know you are past words. Past reason.

The ground starts to grind and shake. You

can hear the storm raging outside, just as it builds inside you. Your wills take on a physical presence of their own. They press against each other, the energy growing into a battle of which the world has never seen, nor will ever see.

Neither of you move, but the world recoils as your soul's clash. Beads of sweat break out on your brow, stinging your eyes and you begin to breath heavily. You both take a step towards each other. As much as you kept your body strong and capable, your mind dulled, while your old friend is sharper than ever. Blood trickles from your nose.

Feeling faint as their will, their resolve, their very mind presses down on yours, you know that if you relent for a moment, it will all be over. The pressure builds, and in a colossal moment you feel them crash down on your mind and soul. You realise that you cannot hold them back any longer. Not like this.

A roar erupts from your mouth as you drive your belt knife into your friend's empty eye socket. Blood spurts over your hand and face, their screech of pain blending with your own scream.

For a moment, your minds are still fighting. But suddenly, your old friend collapses, and the overwhelming pressure that was about to break your mind abruptly evaporates. There is no time for sadness or grief. In a twist of fate, your own mind, now suddenly unresisted, is flung into the eternal universe.

Your mind reaches out to grab something, anything to anchor you to the physical world. A warm but wild connection is made, but it also detaches with you from reality. Darkness encloses, leaving your mind drifting beyond the world.

An instantaneous eternity ensues. You have no concept of time. No sensation guides your body of its passage. You realise you have lost your mind. It is gone, left to wander the cosmos. You can only hope a beacon will light the way back to your body, to the comfort of reality. The sensation of eternity continues until light slowly unfolds and you realise you are back in a different body, one that feels old and broken. You realise you're not alone.

Your eyes slowly open, the ambient light reveals a dark place of black bars, the feel of cold iron surrounding you. It is a cage, thrown into a corner of a room that smells of rot and mould and death. A tall dark figure stands before you outside the cage, their robed hands enfolding a walking stick of bone placed neatly in front of them. Their face is darkly veiled and their voice rasps painfully to your ears.

"You live. Then the task had best be done."

You try to speak, but instead a coughing fit takes hold. Words escape from your cracked lips in a croak, leaping forth to express your need to please the creature before you.

"Yes, your Eminence, their ... their presence is gone from the world, so that you may continue to be the glory of all. It is done as you wished."

They tilt their head as if calculating your existence, like you are a mangey dog that has performed a trick. Not because the trick was amusing, but because you did as they commanded.

Slowly and deliberately, they walk away. They do not need to justify themselves. No explanation will be forthcoming to you. The only thing that concerns them is being able to continue exerting their will on the world. It's a wonder that you and your caged family are even alive, after years of having to project a false reality on your old friends mind from inside a cage. There must be more they require of you. Will they ever free you and your family as promised?

Time passes hazily. You sit there questioning if things could have been different, if you should have helped your old friend instead of being the instrument of their final demise. You look down at your withered and tear-stained hands, at the note that sits there, now dirty, torn, and blooded.

You look around at the other cages. Your family. The dim light that cascades from cracks in the ceiling barely illuminates the faces of your loved ones. No words are spoken by them, but words from an ancient voice fill your mind, "It's not too late."

Light bursts awake in front of you, a flame consuming the note in your hands. You manage to stare into it, seeing the creature of the void that is the flame. The Fire Spirit from the cave. It's voice reverberates through your soul, "You are not finished. There is work to be done yet."

The End ... for now.

Death's Hall

All is silent in the Halls of the Dead,
Where dead men's music
Falls,
Upon the loving tears of the dearly departed.
Shimmering shadows watch over the
lamented
As the notes of the enlightened
Linger,
And the song of death's final melody
Signals the Reaper's return.

Maybe life is fragile so that we may know the value of it.

However, life is also just a matter of perspective.

You just have to embrace the adventure of finding your own.

For you, blank pages. Feel free to explore your own travelling mind!

For the Travelling Mind

Chased by Demons

I can smell the blood that covers the leather interior of my Mercedes sedan. All I hear is the screaming wail of Demons, reverberating off the dark high-rises that envelop me as I drive.

They continue chasing me through the city, present at every turn. I hope, even pray, that they get distracted by someone else. Just leave me for a new victim. Maybe there's a small chance that I can lose them before I get to the hospital.

So much blood. It's not my blood, but I wish it were. My son quietly sitting next to me, is clearly in pain. His fear palpable on his pale face, and his dazed look of worry wrenches at my soul. The dark viscous fluid covers everything, even blending with the tears that stream down my face.

I should have seen the Demons for what they were. But they found us and caused all this to happen. Maybe my boy would be whole – not bleeding out beside me through the makeshift bandage I made before getting in the car. If only I knew how, I would fix him myself. Saved him myself. But there's still hope! I just have to get to the hospital.

With a sharp turn to the right, I cut through traffic, frustrated that it seems to always get in the way. I then swerve, trying to hit one of the Demons as they point a pistol at me from the edge of the road. Curse it for diving out of the way! They just seem to be everywhere. I turn down another street, this time to the left.

I put my foot to the floor, the V8 engine roaring as I dodge around traffic on both sides of the road. A clear stretch of road opens up before me and the sound of the Demons' wails seems to be getting further away. I might just have a chance yet. From memory the hospital is only two or three blocks away. I turn another corner at speed, causing the car to drift. Excitement rushes through me and I start to feel hopeful. I might get my son there in time, I'm so close!

I look down at my boy, his eyes starting to glaze as they stare fixedly at the dashboard in front of him. My heart withers and panic sets in. Unbidden, signals from my brain to my foot make me stamp my foot down on the accelerator. Looking up through the windows, I notice that the Demons are crawling all over the place, especially on the road in front of the emergency department of the hospital. I cannot let them stop me. I have to get inside so I can save him. Even if it kills me.

I steer the car towards the side road that leads to the door of the emergency depart-ment. I hold onto my boy beside me as I slam on the brakes at the last minute, and we come to a complete stop. His chest is heaving long and ragged breaths. He still lives. Thank God he is still breathing at all. I undo his seatbelt and drag him out through my side of the car door.

In a hurry, I throw him over my shoulder and draw my pistol. I look up and I see all the demons are starting to advance with weapons drawn. I yell and scream for them to get back. They screech and roar in return. I fire a few shots at them, causing one to drop to the ground and the rest of them to scatter and dive out of the way. I know that they will not return fire from where they stand for risk of shooting into the building. The truce within the hospital grounds forbids them from doing so.

I race through the department doors, yelling for someone to help, but the only person there is a young girl with big brown eyes hiding behind the glass of the counter. I shout at her to help me, but I can see that she is too scared. The Demons must have never been so close to her before.

Full of fear she musters up her courage, telling me that they can help him, but no one is allowed out to get him until I leave. Curse these Demons chasing me! I roar in rage. I gently put my son down, infuriated that I am here but can't do anything for him in what could be his final moments. I tell her I will leave, that I will deal with the Demons that are outside. The ones who let this happen.

The waiting room is still empty as I turn to face the doors. I can see the Demons regrouping behind my car on the other side of the glass doors, screeching in blood lust. Taking aim, I shoot my way through the doors before they have a chance to open. The Demons take cover. I become the calm rage of death. Like Roland of Gilead, I gather my focus, unleashing lead upon my enemies.

I continue firing away as I step outside onto the pavement. Bullets crash about me, as casings bounce and clatter all over the ground from both sides. The Demons are fighting back with their screams, as some of their weapons go unused. I may yet defeat them and return to my child's side. I hope and pray that he will be saved.

Distracted by the thought of him, I turn to check inside. Are they seeing to him? Suddenly shots ring out to the left of me. I feel my flesh torn all over and my chest erupts with pain and blood. My pistol explodes out of my shattered hand, clattering to the ground as my breath is taken from me. I try to look back around, but I cannot see the Demon who did this. Instead, I find myself staring up at the lights on the ceiling of the entryway.

My body goes deathly cold, and my vision starts to tunnel. A sad but friendly faced police officer comes into view. I try to tell him that they were too late, but no words come out as I reach out to him. He takes my hand, putting his other hand on my chest before looking around and yelling commands. But I cannot hear his words. I can no longer see him clearly, but in this moment, I am just grateful that the police defeated the Demon that killed me.

I kneel down beside the man now lying on the ground, ignoring the blood pooling around him. I place my gloved hand on his chest, putting pressure on his gunshot wound. I take his out-stretched hand with my other hand as he tries to say something, but I just cannot make it out. His face is already going slack, and his hand limp.

I cut the man's shirt off with my trauma sheers and call out to the other police officers to get the paramedics and hospital staff. Pulling out a chest seal from my personal medical kit, I place it over the entry wound to the man's chest, in the hope it will prevent the lungs from completely collapsing. Even though the man wounded two of our officers, we still have an obligation to try save him.

My colleague, Belinda, comes up next to me with tears in her eyes. We both look down at the man, and I cannot help but feel sad for her. She was the one who shot this maniac. Only a few months on the job and she has already taken someone's life. But she was brave for moving up and flanking the man to fire on him. We all wanted to take a shot, but from our position we could not risk shooting into the hospital. From our angle, we could have potentially hit one of the staff, or even the man's boy who had to lay there until the father was neutralised.

The paramedics and hospital staff come out from everywhere and take away the wounded police and the man on the ground. I stand there in a daze for a moment. How could this man let his life get to this point? The thought of it makes my hair stand on end. Taking me out of my torpor, a triage nurse motions for me to come with her, her big brown eyes understanding. No one seems to need me right now, so I follow her inside.

We walk through the waiting room. Glass covers the floor of the entry way, and a patch of blood can be seen in front of the nurse's desk. She makes me sit down in an office and hands me a cup of water. I have no words as I take it from her, tears falling from my eyes. My body starts trembling all over. All I can think about is the madman, of how that could have been me. That it could have been my son.

The Coroner's report stated that the man had been under the influence and suffered a drug induced psychosis. Detectives tell me that he had turned his pistol on his wife for no known reason, not realising his son was behind her. She, unfortunately, died at the scene. If the boy survives, he will never see his parents again.

I could have been the madman. If not for seeking help and getting my life in order, I realise that could have been me. Tonight, I will hug my family so tight, forever thankful that I changed who I was, that I rescued myself from my own demons.

Hearts Apart

This poem, from thy Heart
Though love I do not profess
It is about our distance apart
And feelings I must confess.

Affection

Desire

Turmoil

Lust holds no place here
Only the want to embrace
To touch, though I fear
A lie, of lust. Just a trace.

Hope

Faith

Pain, inflicted upon thyself
From unrealised aspirations
And expectations of yourself
Become failed reparations.

Love

It comes in different ways
In family, strangers, and friends
Over years or instantly, it strays
But in time, and on us, it all depends.

Language, expressed as poetry,
can capture a moment in time
in such a way that's unlike
anything else in this world.

A Nurse's Reflection

I did not really know the old man and unfortunately, I can't remember exactly why he was in hospital at that point. But I do remember how his eyes lit up briefly, along with his toothless smile. Oh, how it made my day. I do not even remember what joke I made, but the moment he started to laugh ... Hell, it may have made my year. It is those small moments when working as a nurse that can make the job worthwhile. Upon reflection, I realise in that shared moment by making the small joke, I had reminded both of us of our humanity, and could tell that I had made him feel more like a normal person instead of just another patient.

It was also eye opening at the time when, being new to working as a nurse, I heard the passing comment from another staff member regarding the same patient. Their experience working there showed, when they sombrely mentioned that he may not survive much longer due to his condition. Days? Weeks? These things are not written in stone for anyone and being a casual nurse with such irregular shifts and unknown locations, I did not get a chance to care for him again. I will never know what happened to him.

At one point the Shifty for the ward came into the room and kindly asked me if I needed help with anything. The irony of this statement was lost on me at the time, however now that I have a moment to think on it, being a casual staff member, I am meant to be there helping them! But I came to learn that help is always appreciated as a nurse, so I kindly agreed to let her assist with the medications.

The most frustrating part of this experience for me was when she realised that I had fallen behind on doing the patients' medication. She went about completing them in half the time it would have taken me. I wanted to be able to do it without help, but the reality is that it took me longer than it did others.

It will always be important to re-educate yourself on what medications are for. If you don't know if you're giving them for the right reasons, it could have significant consequences. Watching the Shifty complete the medications so quickly and confidently was inspiring, but also embarrassing. At the time, I quietly thanked her for her help. Her understanding speaks volumes of her compassion, as she expressed her own gratitude that I was there at all. Bless her.

What is endearing, is that at the time she understood it was not my regular job and was happy to help me throughout the shift. It makes me appreciate that I've had the opportunity to work with such people. It does, when you meet that one jaded staff member. This actually happened on the same shift. They not so politely alluded to the uselessness of casual staff, and even the other staff members in general. It is a terrible attitude to have, however, I understand their frustration.

As a new casual nurse, it always felt like starting from scratch, with login issues, extra paperwork to fill, machines to access but then needing other people to organise it. These processes all add up, taking up time that could be spent treating. That doesn't even include having to learn who the patients are, where things are located and sometimes even looking up what certain medical conditions are, so that we can keep on track of how we are to best care for our patients.

I was sitting in the staff room sometime later, being an hour overdue taking my break, contemplating my life. It is a lot sometimes, knowing that I was spending my Sunday working to maintain clinical experience and get ahead of my finances, when I could have been sitting by the beach, out experiencing nature, or spending time with friends. The joys of being conscientious!

To think that I had felt hard done by some days when it was my own fault. A friend once told me I am the common denominator in all my problems. I wonder if that is a condition of my generation, or even just society. When we feel that working above and beyond for our own sense of accomplishment, that somehow, we are entitled to more. But really, people have their own lives to get on with. They are not always concerned with what other people are doing in their own time. And why should they be?

Maybe I am generalising like I always do, but I guess I was in this boat with all the other staff members here. To throw out some platitudes and aphorisms: We are where we are by our own choice, and it is up to us to make something of it. Really, perspective is everything in life.

Sitting in the tearoom, I sighed as my coffee must have finished minutes ago, which was a good indicator that my break was over.

I groaned as I stood, getting myself ready to face the last half of my shift. I began to think that as much as I was qualified to work as a nurse, it was also overwhelming.

Cleaning up my cup and plate, I thought of all the other jobs I have done in the past, and how they compare to being a nurse. Returning to the floor, I thought about the constant challenges that I faced in my current fulltime job. Challenged by things such as medical training while fatigued, conducting group physical training, interpersonal relations, or just doing superfluous administrative work that always ran the risk of being sent back for inconsequential errors. They are things that are difficult or frustrating to deal with, but not in the same ways that I had experienced working in a hospital. It does not matter though when we get paid right? Somethings in life just do not compare.

Again, my thoughts were distracted. Moving back to the hospital work, patient cares took up a lot of time for the rest of the shift. Simple things like making sure that they got to the toilet so that they did not soil themselves in their beds. So simple, but so important.

Most of the job, in case you were not aware, includes things like making beds and constant cleaning and recording vital signs, (blood pressure, breathing rate, heartrate, and temperature). Such simple things to make sure patients were as well they could be, by identifying any small changes that can indicate to us any deterioration due to their medical condition.

Remember, if it's not documented, it never happened. In the eyes of the legal system anyway. There was, and will always be a lot to consider, made all the more difficult when you are away from the work. Skill fade can become a serious problem.

Again! My thoughts trailed off while I helped reposition the lovely little old lady in bed. She came in for treatment related to blood pressure and a broken wrist, as she had suffered a fall at home related to her blood pressure levels being out of whack. I think it was heart related, but I had not had a chance to have a look at her full history or recent electrocardiogram. To be honest, I barely had the time to learn about her past history due other work that needed to be done. It could also easily be confused with another patient who presents with the same or similar conditions. I still made the effort to double check her notes to aid in understanding how to best care for her.

At the end of the day, what I remember most is that she was an absolute delight to look after. Her banter game was strong as she dished out wit without holding back. Her husband came in to see her and with skipping a beat, joined in as if he had been there from the start.

He never said it, but I had a feeling he appreciated how we cared for his wife. His appreciation was only given away through brief smiles and quiet thanks. Concern and affection for his wife was subtle but apparent from the way he looked at her when she wasn't looking, and his keen attention to what was going on around him. Under the smiles and laughs we had, was a man who cared and loved his wife, and who unwittingly showed appreciation for our attempts to provide comfort in such a gloomy place. But again sadly, I may never know what happened to the patients I have cared for.

There is so much more to reflect upon from that shift. From any shift actually. One last thing I will mention though, is the difficulty of not letting emotions, or feelings regarding patients or work colleagues, get to you beyond what could be considered healthy. Reflecting in them is important, but toxic when held onto unnecessarily. I imagine that this will always continue to challenge me. The constant juxtapositions of smiles and tears, life and death, will ever be present in the job and leave their mark.

Hopefully, having experienced these things, I will continue developing and bettering myself. And maybe by investing in these moments shared with other souls, in a place where we all are challenged ... I hope that maybe I have at least given them some comfort.

Scent of a New World

Shade and sun cover my face
As I walk along this dirt path
Trees all around, a breeze carrying ...
Carrying scents of life, the world.

Content, I continue until the sun
Beams fully down upon me, the heat
Rejuvenating, the breeze refreshing. The
Green undergrowth, beneath Ancient giants
Looming above, with limbs extending and
Intertwining. The smaller scrub beneath, like
Vibrant green children.

The Path ends, a sudden fork.
No breeze, a clouded sun
Which way to go?
The giants and children go anxiously

Still. I contemplate my decision, left, or right?
Fate is hanging in this moment . . .
Sweat stands out on my forehead, my hands
Open and close as I assess and calculate,
Both Path's seem the same,
Which way to go?

Coin tossed, it spins, spins, spins for
Eternity. Heads. Dissatisfied I take the tails
Path, my own tail tucked between my legs.
The Sun opens up, the breeze smells new
Giants sway along and Children laugh.

Shade and sun cover my face
As I walk along this dirt path
Trees all around, a breeze carrying ...
Carrying scents of life, the world.
Troubled I continue as the sun goes

Dark. The breeze, once refreshing is now
Chilly. The looming giants brace themselves
The children begin to weep, the sap
Red. I think, as all takes on a quality like
Decay. Why was it so hard to make the
Decision? It never crosses my mind to go back
To be able to try again just does not happen
Fate is hanging . . .

The forest clears and a Bridge comes into
View. A chasm underneath, on either
Side. To the left, a drop with no
Bottom. To the right, a cliff face with no
Top. In the distance, peaceful fields stretching
Away. The world stops; life holds its breath.
The wooden Bridge, rickety and long
Is everything foreboding?

Fear grips me. Scared to make a mistake, I
Procrastinate, with deliberation
Striking me still.
Seeking a way out, suddenly, I find
Inspiration. To take a leap of faith.
I step back, rush forward and I
Leap ... no I fly! Soaring out into
Space. A mighty jump, to clear the
Bridge. I make it and fields await!

I look back, reflecting on my
Trials. See how far I have come? I have
Achieved. Turning to the fields awaiting, Elated,
Ecstatic, my joy and smile fade to
Dust. The fields are now barren, and
Dark. No life, no peace. Tranquillity is
Forgotten. Only ash and the departed.
Why? What went wrong?

To think that the Bridge had stopped me, nay,
Subdued me. I question. But It I overcame! I
Pause, feeling the Dead's eyes boring into my
Soul. A corpse at my feet, stares at me. In a
Whisper, Death's voice screamed,
THIS IS THE PRICE WE PAY.

Perhaps the bridge had not stopped me. In
Fear of being challenged, I missed the
Journey. I see now, I did not learn.
Shame and disappointment abound, as
Shade and sun cover my face.
I walk along this new dirt path
Emptiness all around, a breeze carrying ...
Carrying scents of a world gone.

Walking through Dead-man's lands
Memories of comforting giants and children
Strong with me. Now gone, this is my price.
Eyes open, I continue through oblivion
Tears and sorrow tearing at my existence.
Still, I close my eyes. Just a trace I can smell
Life, an uplifting breeze caressing my
Skin. It is no dream! A scent of a new
World. Maybe my tears will never stop
Falling, on all that is around me. As I have
Learned, I will explore the world, in the
Moment, with my tears irrigating the
Earth, bringing forth new life. With it, the
Scent of a New World.

A Respectful Conversation

Of all the influential people
That I have met in life
Only one has left with me
A resounding statement.

His speech reflects life's lessons
Because that is how he is.
When I mentioned to him
How respectful he was to all.

He replied, and I paraphrase,
"It is an important thing
To remember,
You can be considerate towards people,
But you can still be
A considerate arsehole."

This struck me as profound and funny.
But I look back
In depth, to consider
Do I act courteously or
Show respect befitting the person?
Or has it all been
The considerations of an arsehole?

Reflecting on his words
Courtesy for all, and
Respect for the individual
Could well be a key foundation
For the good in humanity.

I write this because strangely
His words left an imprint
And I feel
Will stick with me
And maybe you
For the rest of my life.

Respect. L. Malone

Learning to listen, instead of waiting for your turn to speak, is no small endeavour. It is challenging.

But the fruit it bears in discussions, make them so much more meaningful.

Draw or write as you wish

Who inspires you dear reader, and why?

Tales of the Ogre and the Wolf

A gentle but icy breeze blew in from the sea, bringing with it the occasional whiff of ocean life, and the distant sound of a bird's cry. The breeze danced across the snowy, barren coastline, and tossed stray drifts of snow about until it was abruptly forced to part ways. The thick skin of an ogre is an impassable thing. This ogre was alone, left to ponder its existence in this inhospitable landscape of white and grey.

Atop a cliff overlooking the sea, the ogre viewed a vast horizon to the east. Day was turning to night and bright stars broke through the bleak sky to wink at the ogre. Sun rays momentarily boasted brilliant reds and yellows from behind her, but they fled as an unforgiving gale herded dark clouds in. The change in the sky, growing winds and churning waves far below reflected the ogre's inner turmoil. She knew how it felt to be chased away. The ogre missed her peaceful forests, untouched by snow or desolation.

Standing three metres tall, bald, and thick browed, she had small black eyes that devoured any light that touched them and an untidy row of fat, round teeth in a large protruding jaw. She was a being of the earth and stone. Big meaty hands extended from arms that resembled logs and, a tree trunk of a chest gave way to a gut that looked made for holding boulders. Its shoulders were as wide as its arms were long. Hard and like rock. Rock covered in scars. No sane creature would try to mess with this ogre.

Forced out from her natural habitat by brutes with forged weapons made to bring down these giants, the ogre was now left to search through desolate lands. Ogres are presumed to be unintelligent, but this is false. They are fast learners and excellent observers, capable of developing skills in uncanny ways.

She took one last look to the east, peering into the turmoil of the sea, before turning inland. Distant and looming mountains wrapped all around, with a gap to the south drawing the eye. The way back home. But not today. She went directly west, towards the foothills and the sun, still trying to peek through clouds over the distant mountains.

The ogre felt lost, like it was halfway to nowhere. The lush forests of the southland she called home were weeks away, and she had no idea what lay ahead. White nothingness covered the surroundings for leagues. Here and there, patches of scraggly rocky fingers sprouted from the snow, and small clusters of weather worn trees broke the monotony of the land. The ogre missed its home, feeling awkward and restless having been gone for months now. She longed for peace again, along with places of warmth and colour, but instead, had to endure this barren world of constant snow and grey.

She continued her rolling gait through the knee-high snow, dreaming of a better place far from this one. Long strong legs carried her far and quickly, with little effort. Without even noticing, the ogre swiftly ploughed through the rolling hills. Surprisingly for their size, ogres don't need to eat much, relying on an omnivore diet to sustain themselves. Thankfully it didn't need to stop for food very often.

Time passed lazily, with only the changing weather to mark its passage. The clouds began a small retreat, egged on by a light breeze. Orange, red, and pink streaks broke through the clouds, showing the tell-tale signs of a pleasant sunset. The encroaching darkness began to pace impatiently while the day was slowly dozing off.

Suddenly, something made the ogre pause and look around. Testing the air with her nose, the ogre picked up the metallic smell of blood in the air. Keen eyes searched the land and found a small, dark grey shape upon the shaded side of the next hill. She cautiously approached. Hidden by the looming rock behind it was an injured wolf. The ogre could smell as much as see that its right hind leg had begun to fester from a vicious wound. The other leg wasn't faring any better and was severely scratched. The wolf growled with a deep thrum when he saw the ogre approach, but the ogre just slowly knelt down by his side.

The wolf bared a bloody, savage grin and then lashed out with his teeth at the ogre's soothing hand. A few beads of blood pearled on the ogre's fingers, but it was an ineffective bite on the wolf's part and the ogre was not phased. Understanding eventually dawned on the wolf as the ogre waited. He finally, hesitantly, licked at the ogre's fingers. The ogre, with surprising gentleness, lifted the wolf's body from the ground, carrying it swiftly to a small clump of trees that could provide a bit of shelter from the biting wind.

Over the next few days, the ogre used what small resources were available to help the wolf. She cleaned his wounds and applied a poultice made from ground roots, and cunningly caught game to feed them. The healing process was as thrilling as watching a turtle move. During this time that the ogre helped the wolf recover, a bond grew, like a small shrub in a desert land, slowly growing and gaining substance under the nurturing light of compassion.

Some days later, the wolf was able to hobble weakly with determination. They eventually decided to head out, the start of their journey together laboured and slow. Sometimes the ogre carried the wolf to ease his aching limbs. Each day more distance was pushed behind them, even as snow and lashing winds battered them. But they continued none-the-less.

Feelings grew in the wolf, and he began to think. His thoughts had always been simple in the way of wolves, but they became more sophisticated as time passed. It was something not experienced before. He found himself drawn to his giant carer. Feelings and thoughts blended to give him a burgeoning sense of duty and purpose. It is like the wolf felt the rising turmoil in the world, his previous need to find his brethren put aside for now so he can help this strange giant. He sensed they might be a part of something greater that would change the world as they knew it.

As the pair travelled, the ogre was coming to the same realisation. Fate was tugging at strings previously untouched, but she also thought Luck was likely to throw dice and interfere with all of Fate's plans, much to the annoyance of Destiny. These three have never been good at co-operating, the ogre thought.

The duo continued their journey west, not knowing exactly where they went. They were essentially following each other without realising it. However, their feet kept going in the direction of the mountains, where woods spread at the base. They were but two insignificant creatures in this vast expanse, but they felt a great sense of purpose. An expectation of things to come, guiding them into the unknown.

To be continued …

Love's Journey

When you are near, my world shakes
When absent, my heart will wait
For you to bring me the water
That offers no quarter
To the thirst that drives
My life to your arms.

When you place your head
Upon my shoulder, I dread
Your leaving face, that tears
My soul when a soft caress
And gentle whisper
Keep me sane at night

Loyalty held straight
Into the jaws that ate
And consumed me whole
Laying me bare upon a soul
Of infinite height into the light
Only to plummet through all

The feeling of pain leaves
Me, under tree's eaves,
With your lips upon my
Mouth, that tastes, so sweet
Makes me believe that
I am full of all things good

Trying to make time, to find
The right piece of mind
Within your soul devouring
Gaze, starts emotions stirring,
A chunk of heart to be shown
To your ever-judging sight
By the moon's face and sun's
Dazzle, God, how it stuns
With heavy memories, the painful
Awareness of the push and pull,
Hinted by distant shores and
Unnatural light shining about us

Stinging words, jests misheard
Creates emotions, feelings stirred
To points of friction, jarring
Against our two minds alike
That want to co-exist
Together in their own worlds

Cravings wished for unfulfilled
And your sombre smile stilled
By unintended actions, confusion
Reigns unfettered, disillusion
Becoming the theme of our lives
That throws us blindly to the wind
To go back to how it was before
Would be a trap, unreal and unsure
As life moves on at its own pace
And our lives together, as individuals
Is too far gone, for us
Is just no longer sustainable

The bitterness fades to history
The anger dissolves within me
To be left alone, nearly forgotten
To live on, a new life so far
From one's kiss, once so sweet
Now only exists, a distant memory.

I was once complaining about a variety of problems to a friend.

She then proceeded to ask, "Have you considered that you are the common denominator in all this?"

This was very enlightening.

Riddle Me Your Dreams

Sleeping, you dream
Awake, you dream
Your life, you dream the day away.

Unseen behind masks, adversaries, self-
claimed allies
Sickly sweet words, disguise tactics designed
to devour
Things falsely fabricated, man-handled by
insecurities.

Procrastinate and clamour for excuses
without knowing
What is cast aside for nothing and with no
consequence
But a missed chance to grow in mind and
worldviews.

Sleeping, you dream
Awake, you dream
Your life, you dream of today

Perceive yourself enclosed by vivid images
in hand
Taunting what you are and where-ever you
stand
Demoralising and attacking your self-
perception.

Enter a dream, thoughts innocent and
optimistic
Only to discover the malevolent hatred of
the weak-minded
Controlling, unnecessary, sinister, and
miserable.

Sleeping, you dream
Awake, you dream
Your life, you dream forever

Awash in thoughts, nod your head in
cognitive dissonance
What you reason to be truth, as dark feelings
stalk
Thoughts, hoping for what is idealistic,
irrational.

Beating savage ideas from suppressed
memories
Into the vulnerable and misunderstanding
child
Of the future; our hero, ourselves.

Sleeping, you dream
Awake, you dream
Your life, you dream of yesterday.

Chase memories of a day, failing to come to
terms
What occurred? To never hear a voice of
reason
A voice that makes us human, to accuse, to
forgive.

A snake on a branch, extends an ideal, a
false gift
To wonder at the snake's existence,
awakened realise
It was all in your own head to begin, and to
end.

Insight enlightens minds once drifting and
lost
Education and work, build foundations
weakened
Perspective expands compassion, constrains
in inexperience

Meaning found in feeling, attention driving
goals
To be driven away from community? No! Be
connected
Don't despair! Light awakens the
slumbering path

Dream of sleeping
Dream of waking
Your life
Your dreams

I am just a simple man.

I do not know where time
comes from

Or where it goes.

All I know is that

It can be found in my watch,

Where it just seems to tick on
by …

And I had better make good
use of it.

The Ogre, the Wolf and the Owl

The vast and snowy woodlands covering the slopes below the mountains were full of life, but only two figures could be seen so brazenly walking through the snow. Sparse flakes fell from a grey bleary sky and on occasion the wind could be heard howling through the crags in the distance above.

The ogre and wolf walked the vast expanses between the large trees of the woods. Not realising they were heading towards a specific point in the distance, it was as if a compass had been guiding them into the mountains all along. Rabbits, foxes, and birds hid from them as they trekked through the cold and white landscape. All sounds were dampened by the thick layer of snow that covered the ground and bare branches above.

From the time they had first met, it had taken the duo several days to travel to where the giant looming trees of the woods could cast a shade on them. The travels had been slow as the wolf recovered from its wounds with the gentle aid of the ogre. Although it was able to walk with a limp, some days require the ogre to carry it when exhaustion set in.

It was not long into the cold afternoon when night suddenly began to fall on the snow-speckled pair. Within moments, the sun disappeared behind the large and looming mountains to the west. The light dimmed and the cold's grip tightened.

Unspoken, they decided to settle in before night did. The wolf, ever vigilant and cautious, snuffled around the small clearing they had stopped at, checking every nook and cranny. The ogre cleared the snow to expose a large patch of fresh dirt under a collection of bushes.

A small sudden huff escaped from the wolf, as he looked up with keen attention towards a snow-covered trail. The ogre turned to the alarming noise and stumbled on an unseen root in the descending darkness. Unphased and confident in dealing with anything, she sat down and made herself comfortable. The wolf quickly looped back around the clearing to the ogre's side, his eyes glowing, a throaty warning growl reverberating through the still, crisp air.

His growl suddenly lowered even further, and he took up a protective stance right before the ogre. An enormous brown bear strolled menacingly into the clearing; its nose held high sniffing the scents in the air. Undeterred by the wolf, the bear faced off to the pair drawing up to its full height, threatening and malevolent.

The ogre gently placed a hand on the wolf's back, making the wolf sit down by her side. She felt confident that she was more likely to survive a conflict with the bear, however even for her, the risks were high in such a cold, unforgiving land.

Frosted breath erupted in the cold air from the bear's mouth, as it released a challenging growl. Worried, the ogre noticed that something was not right about the bear. It shook its head, and pawed at itself, seemingly suffering from an internal struggle. The bear straightened up, forepaws swiping wildly in the air. Crashing down onto all fours, its loud roar ripped through the quiet of the woods. It charged at the pair.

Suddenly, out of the dark treetops darted a brilliant blur of white and grey, right into the face of the charging bear. In fury, the bear swiped its massive paws and attempted to bite at the indistinct shape but could not be rid of the mass flittering about its head.

After only a few seconds, the bear's face was bloodied, and it became apparent to the onlooking duo that it was no longer able to see. The bear became defensive and tried to protect its face as it withdrew from the barrage of attacks. In blind rage, it turned and ran headfirst into a tree, causing a heap of snow and small branches to fall to the ground. Stunned only for a moment, it awkwardly ambled away into the dark woods.

As the bear disappeared out of sight, the blur of white and grey slowed momentarily to reveal an owl, her large, frenzied eyes glistening in the low light of the evening. She continued to zoom about the clearing, head and eyes darting about to lock onto anything that moved.

Languidly, the ogre stood and meandered towards the sounds of the owl's shenanigans. In a tentative but precise motion, the ogre put out one of its gnarly hands and caught the owl mid-air. The bird screeched, the distressing sound lingering in their ears even after it had stopped.

The wolf hobbled over in panic, as a stray feather drifted down to blend with the ground. The ogre and the wolf locked eyes for a second, and the wolf watched on as the ogre opened its hand enough to reveal the owl looking around, its eyes taking in the two. She twisted and squirmed, but eventually realised the ogre was not going to let it out.

Curiosity piqued, the owl calmed down and peered through the ogre's fingers. She let out a couple quiet hoots, gently pecking at the ogre's tough fingers. The ogre slowly opened up her hand, releasing the owl. She stayed in the ogre's hand for a moment before hopping up to its massive shoulder. Continuing to quietly hoot, it looked pointedly between the ogre and the wolf.

To the wolf's surprise, the owl jumped down onto his back then the ground, her white form blending with the snow. Her hoots persisted, encouraging the pair to follow as she hopped up the hill in the direction the bear had come from. After a moment, the wolf nudged the ogre and let her gently place her hand on his back to guide her through the darkness of the woods.

In the general quietness of the frosty night air surrounding them, the tiniest of sounds seemed all the louder. The crack of a stick, scattered drops of ice-water and the faint whistle of wind in the treetops punctuated the night. Through the cold, the wolf and ogre followed the owl's vague shape and soft hoots.

Out of the blue night, a black void arose in front of them, dark and ominous. The air stilled and earthy smells of damp dirt and lichen filled their nostrils. Sight momentarily escaped even the wolf and they had to trust the owl to guide them. As their eyes adjusted to the darkness a cave took shape around them. The owl alighted on the ogre's shoulder, gently pecking, and hooting. Cradling the owl in her hands, the ogre sat down against the far wall. The wolf looked out into the darkness from the cave's entrance, checking for danger one last time.

Satisfied, he settled down beside the other two, sleep quickly claiming them.

A light blue haze greeted them as they arose and moved out into the still morning. From the elevated height of the cave entrance, they could see through the branches of the skeletal trees down to the plains and distant ocean in the east. The sun, bright but not yet warming, peaked out from over the horizon. Unbidden, the wolf's hackles bristled forth, and the others' gaze followed the wolf's. Some distance below, they could see, following behind, the massive brown shape of a bear.

The owl hooted, sharp and low, as it skittered above from branch to branch. She set off west, further into the mountains behind them, and they followed. It was not long until they lost sight of the bear. Despite that, urgency quickened their steps. With a sense of rightness, they continued to follow the owl.

Light snow drifted from the sky throughout the morning. As they hiked their way into the mountains, the path became a steep rocky trail. The trees thinned out, replaced by snow covered bushes and bare outcrops. Where they could, the owl and wolf snacked on field mice and other small prey, while the ogre foraged for withered berries, roots, and plants.

The owl, fatigued, took roost on the ogre's shoulder, while the gentle giant smoothly navigated the steep rocky slopes. The wolf's hackles stirred again, and he looked back along their path on the precipitous slope. The bear was slowly gaining on them. With a glance at the others, the wolf turned and continued the climb.

Suddenly, he slipped as he leaped towards a ledge to get around a boulder. His yelp rang out, causing the owl to wake. The wolf landed at the ogre's feet and was unable to stand again as his injured leg gave out. There was a slight rumble from above them and the ground shook.

The rumbling grew and a worried screech burst from the owl as the ogre threw her high in the air. With her other hand, she grabbed the wolf and tossed him into the shelter of the ledge above. Snow and rock cascaded down, the avalanche flowing past and over the wolf to bombard the ogre in an impressive cloud of white.

Everything settled and went quiet. A thick layer of snow teetered on the lip of the ledge the wolf sat under. The ogre had disappeared. In a light puff of snow, the owl landed in front of the wolf and frantically started to dig around. The wolf joined in but was severely hampered by his injury. The pair, unable to get very far down, revealed nothing but snow and rock.

Exhausted and disheartened by their lack of progress, they stopped and stared solemnly at the small hole they had dug. The light snow continued to fall, and the sun overhead provided little warmth. The two began to worry, their urge to move on growing. It felt wrong to leave the gentle giant behind, but what else could they do?

The sun was fast approaching the mountains, prompting them to continue on and find shelter while it was still bright. It was slow going and tedious, grief and fatigue wearing them down. Just before dark fell, they nestled into a wide crack within the mountain. In their shelter the wind no longer cut through them, and freezing water trickled down the walls, quenching their thirst.

On the verge of sleep, the wolf heard a noise coming from outside. The owl slept undisturbed on the wolf's back as he looked up. Nothing could be seen through the light grey wall of snow outside. He sniffed at the cold wet air, but the wind outside carried away anything that would give him a clue. Sounds of heavy footsteps grew. Could it be that the bear had finally caught up with them? The wolf stood up, causing the owl to roll off and screech in surprise, agitated at being woken up.

The wolf backed up and took an aggressive stance. Eventually the owl realised something was wrong and hid behind him. They could only hope that whatever it was might overlook them, as their backs were literally against a wall. The grey emptiness of the entrance darkened as an indistinct shape came into view. Hunkered down, the owl looked out from behind the wolf, twitching its wings and claws in preparation to fight.

A scent, just a hint, from the new arrival made it to the wolf's nose. Startling the owl, the wolf suddenly got up and hobbled over as the battered and bruised ogre stepped into the crack. The ogre drank briefly from the trickling ice-water on the wall, before turning and embracing the wolf. With an embarrassed smile, she dumbly pointed to a nasty cut and bump on top of her head. The owl landed on the ogre's shoulder, hooting loudly in joy.

The trio spent the night undisturbed as the snow came and went in drifts in front of their den. Morning arrived and they drank the water that continued to run down the wall before heading off. They slowly climbed further into the mountains, the owl scouting out food which, although not filling, was enough to sustain them.

After several trips, the owl returned with a handful of small berries for the ogre, clearly distressed. With urgent hoots, it indicated to look down the hill. They peered back the way they came, to see the bear was catching up. Its ruined face and matted fur made the ogre concerned about what could be driving this sad creature.

The ogre again carried the wolf and the owl, their pace slow on the treacherous ground. Groans of pain and exhaustion escaped her lips. Morning turned to afternoon as they carried on. Rocks, dirt, and snow disappeared into crevices that they had to navigate around, but the ogre always managed to nimbly leap out of the way. And yet the bear followed, ever present.

A snowstorm fell upon them, making it impossible to see beyond the ogre's out-stretched hand. Try as they might, no rock outcrop or ledge provided them with enough cover, forcing them to press on with tiny steps and slow deliberate movements over the ever-treacherous ground.

Abruptly, the chaos of the storm turned into complete blackness. All was still. No snow. No wind. No crevices. Just infinite, flat and seamless ground. It was eerily quiet, their small movements echoing into nothing-ness. Except for the black, glass-like reflec-tion of the floor, foggy darkness encircled them. Somehow, they were still able to see each other clearly. The owl climbed up to the ogre's shoulder, and when the wolf was placed on the ground, his shape was reflected back at him.

The wolf took a step. With a resounding thud, a stone slab twice the size of the ogre appeared in front of them. All three looked at each other in confusion. For a minute no one moved while they appraised the slab. The owl sneezed as the ogre stepped closer and scratched her head, eyes darting over the hundreds of glyphs on the hard surface. Hooting excitedly, the owl pointed her wing at an engraving that resembled her own feathers. The ogre carried them both close enough that the owl was able to reach out and touch the engraving.

The owl vanished. The ogre frowned and the wolf froze in panic. The silence stretched out and nothing further happened. There was no temperature change, but the wolf shivered none-the-less.

The ogre scratched her head again, scrutinising the glyphs even further. She recognised some as creatures or plants, but many of the symbols were confusing and unknown. She determined that they told a story, but it did not make sense to her. One glyph stood out at the ogre's hip height, hind legs of a wolf within the shape of a canine tooth. She glanced down at the wolf who was distracted looking around the surrounding void, as if the owl had just gone for a flight.

The air shuddered in front of the ogre as she took a deep breath. With grim resolve, she gently grabbed the wolf's tail and made it touch the glyph of the leg and tooth. The wolf whipped his head around, a look of horror on his face an instant before vanishing.

The ogre sighed and rubbed her face, before looking again at the stone wall, eyes baggy and face worn. Further inspection revealed nothing to her, and she sat down to rest with her back against the stone.

The passage of time was lost for the ogre while she sat there, eyes closed. A feeling of unease eventually woke her, a disturbing presence in the surrounding void made her look about. Her gaze fell on the torn weeping stare of the brown bear, which appeared only a few paces away.

The bear charged, maw drooling and carrion stench filling the air a moment before crashing into the stone wall where the ogre was. She frantically rolled out of the way just in time. The bear turned to attack, its head making contact again with the wall, just to vanish as the others had.

Standing quickly, the ogre ran her hands over the glyphs in desperation, but nothing happened. She tried again to no avail. Tears flowing, she moved around to the other side of the wall. There, in the centre, was a single glyph. Three miniature versions of herself, holding hands to make a circle. It seemed more real engraved into the rock than anything she had ever seen. A quiet moan escaped her lips, and she reached out, caressing the glyph. Darkness engulfed her, and she vanished.

Have a thought? Is something troubling you?
Write it down and get it off your mind.

Tides of the New Age

Memories distantly break upon the shores of
subconsciousness.
Thoughts within the whirlpools of avarice
and confused understanding.
Privileged and conflicting ideals drown
uplifting voices of intangible worlds.
Misleading truths, judgemental faces and
the emotionless confound us.
Demon masked objects swirl within the lives
of disgruntled shapes of society.

Powerful tides consume the unsuspecting
with instant gratification.
Swells of change crash, shaping possibilities
of individuality, of civilisation.
Scintillating surfaces flash and reflect the
glamour others want us to see.

Walk on wet sand, to become brainwashed
by misleading information.
Floating on currents of currency, humanity
is swept away, leaving but a shell.

Swimming through meaningless
comprehension, we question existence.
Drifting between object and idea, to be
brought crashing into the claws of
discontent.
Sweeping, oppressing and powerful, the
waves move us all.
As all flows into the oceans of technology,
where will we be left stranded?

I sometimes think that humanity lives in the future so much so, that it is more real and attainable than we even realise … Except Elon Musk. He probably has a good idea.

Jetpacks

This jetpack is pretty cool. It looks fancy and sleek with flash copper highlights against the black painted framework. The important part about this model, is that it has a better particle accelerator than the last. At the same time, this jetpack was modified to blend with the helmet and lightly armoured suit, so it all looks like some sleek, futuristic mechatronic suit. Even just the idea of it thrills me. It is no Iron Man suit, but it is the closest thing going, and it is just awesome.

Cruising through the air, my integrated helmet tells me on the heads-up display, that the pressure from the acceleration acting on my suit is reaching its resistance limit. The last model didn't get to that point, which means this latest breakthrough is really going to give this product an edge over our competition.

In a moment of clarity, I pause to admire the clear blue sky and the ground far below me. Oh, how I appreciate this part of the job, and I laugh to myself considering that people still pay out their arse just to experience what I do for a living. An alert goes off, interrupting my thoughts. Damn, I'm near the edge of my approved airspace and practically have to backflip to avoid going beyond it. Time to return and complete the next test.

I glide up higher into the sky and complete a long wide loop so that I'm completely upside down. With gravity assisting me, I get an even larger thrill as I head straight for the bright white sands of the beach below. It feels glorious, exhilarating and like I might shit myself, but I manage to refrain from doing so. Pride and professionalism aside, it would make quite a mess of the suit. Half-way through the controlled descent, the engine suddenly cuts out and I lose all power. I might shit myself after all.

The people gathered on the beach pointing up at me. I can also distantly hear their screams as they realise that my power has cut out and I am starting to spiral into a completely uncontrolled decent. That is fair. I would do the same if I were in their shoes. What a way to die, plummeting to the ground in front of everyone. No doubt they all have their smart glasses streaming the whole event too, and I suppose I would not have it any other way.

I get to a height where, with the aid of my helmet, I am able see their individual details. It makes me happy knowing how good the picture comes up, the view amplified by my helmet. Is that kid frozen in the motion of picking his nose? Go figure.

As the screams of concern get louder, and people start to run away from where they expect me to crash, the Save-me function kicks in. Small jets located near my shoulders and hips jerk me back into a nearly upright position. The sudden force of the velocity change sends a crushing wave of nausea through me, right before I crumple to the ground on my right side, my jostled head knocking me unconscious.

Moments later, I regain consciousness with a throbbing headache, opening my eyes to see sand and people's feet not far from me. Shit, everything hurts, especially my right side. Suddenly, I feel small pricks in the skin of my back, and within moments, a wave of relief flows over me. The receding pain confirms for me the final test I had to do on the suit.

I didn't, however, envisage it would happen this way. Breathing awkwardly, I manage to sigh in relief at still being alive. I slowly roll onto my stomach, finding that my body works, with no breaks. Not that anyone can see through my helmet, I smile in triumph and joy at my success.

Stiff, nauseated and still sore, I stand up. I then throw my hands in the air, both in jubilation and to show the crowd that I am okay. They awkwardly clap, except for the kid I saw just before the landing who is still dumbly staring at me with his previously occupied finger forgotten in front of his face. It makes me laugh and I realise it does not matter. I feel ecstatic!

My work colleague Celeste bursts through the crowd, giving me an enthusiastic hug. Her red hair is streaming about her smiling, freckled face as she steps away and points to her integrated glasses and media orb in her other hand.

In a slightly shaky but excited voice she says "Are you okay? You are standing, so that's good! So ... I got the whole thing from this view and some with the media orb even though I had a small connection problem for a moment. The flight and tumble should come up great, although the landing looked rougher than I was expecting. But it worked just as we hoped ... I mean expected ha-ha. How do you feel?"

She awkwardly laughs but I cannot get the big smile off of my face as I say, "I think that one of the counter thrusters at my hip was out of calibration. It would explain the landing. I'm a bit sore but otherwise I feel great! I gathered a lot of data, and it looks like this model is going to blow the last one out of the air. Ha-ha, pun not intended ... but if we get the manufacturing approval, I think this is going to be a big break for us. I'm glad we're working together on this; we make a great team."

I notice that for a fraction of a second her smile wavers, but without skipping a beat she says, "This is going to be so exciting to see launch! Let's head back to the workshop and look at the data while we edit the videos."

Normally after field tests, we would grab a drink and discuss our next set of plans. This time however, my excitement is nearly overwhelming, and I forget the idea of going for drinks in favour of doing more work. My hands shaking from the surge of adrenaline,

I take off my helmet and wave to the crowd. I utter some vague words of thanks and tell them to keep on the lookout for future product release events.

We get to our white work-van, and I begin unsuiting in the back so I can get back into regular clothes. It is an easy but slightly time-consuming process. I hear Celeste's muffled voice from the front cab and assume she has received a call. Halfway through taking apart the suit I finally hear a second voice. I guess it is just one of the on lookers who has come up to ask some questions, as I struggle slightly with one of the boot clips. I always forget to take the boots off first ...

Alternate Endings 

The Intriguing Plot – Page 111

The Hopeless Romantic Plot – Page 132

The Lost Plot – Page 168

The Intriguing Plot

... Suddenly the back doors open, and I yell in embarrassment. The light blinds me momentarily as I attempt to make out the silhouette standing in front of me. Well ... I make an effort to figure out who the person is, except the blinding daylight and having an assault rifle promptly shoved in my face makes it difficult. I quickly forget my attempt to figure out who it is, the barrel being so close that I can smell the metal.

In that split second, the only details I can make out is that their clothes are dirty and tattered, like they have been living rough for a while. A beard and long hair disguises most of their face but I can just see from their silhouette that they are wearing integrated glasses that look a lot like Celeste's.

Their raspy, deep masculine voice is full of tension and panic as they make their demands, "Hand over the jetpack and suit, fuckwit. I ain't joking, this is loaded and if you don't hurry up, I'll shoot you *and* ya friend. Now! All of it."

His yelling violently prompts me into action, and I frantically continue taking off the remainder of the suit. Panic makes it even harder than usual, my fine motor skills gone. My voice breaks on me as I shout, "Stop yelling at me, I'm doing it … My stupid boot is stuck … There! Take it, just stop pointing the gun at me!"

Awkwardly sitting in the back of the van in my underwear, I watch this guy stuff my suit into a duffle bag. As he puts the suit in the bag, the barrel of the rifle continues to wave all over the place. It smacks me in the face as he leans over to grab the jetpack itself. I try not to shit myself again for the second time today. I would be less concerned about his gun discipline, except that he has had his finger on the trigger the whole time.

He puts the jetpack in a separate bag and slings it over his shoulder, glaring at me. His bright green eyes burn into my soul and his voice is full of anger as he yells, "Fuck you!"

He viciously kicks the doors shut, and I can hear his footsteps as he runs off. His dishevelled body now out of sight, I sit there dazed. Did I know that maniac? The pain left from his gun and the suddenness of it all makes it hard for me to process the situation. I finally stick my head out the back, in time to see him jump into a car down the road and drive off in a massive screech of tires.

Remembering Celeste, I grab my jeans and hop into them as I go around to the front of the car to check on her. I do not realise I am yelling as I say, "Celeste, this guy just took the jetpack and suit. This is going to ruin … oh you're crying. What's wrong?"

Muffled by her hands covering her face, as

she says "Sam you jerk! He just robbed me as well! He seemed so hard done by, I felt sorry for him, and then he shoved the gun in my face and took my glasses and, and the Media Orb, then called me a stupid bitch and ran away. I heard him yelling at you, but I was so scared I couldn't move."

I don't know how to respond but I can feel my disbelief evaporate as reality takes hold of me, a seething rage building in me. How dare this guy take all my hard work away from me? Something stirs in the back of my memory, but I shove it as a plan starts to form in my mind. Out loud I say, "It will be fine, he'll get what's coming."

She opens her mouth to speak but I've already turned away, focusing on my next move. I walk back around to the rear of the van and jump in, turning on the small touch screen computer that connects to the tools we use to run diagnostics and fine tune components of the jetpack. Conveniently, I had set up remote access so that I did not have to have the suit on to run it. Also having installed GPS tracking for airspace permit reasons, it only takes seconds for me to find the location of all the gear. I bring it up on the small hand-held screen in front of me and start protocols to redistribute the power outlets of the particle accelerator in the jetpack.

Celeste gets in the back with me, still sniffling and wiping her tears. Giving her an encouraging smile, I turn back to the screen, attempting to figure out where they might be taking the equipment. After a moment of her looking over my shoulder she gasps and says, "Are you doing what I think you are?! Why don't you just call the police and let them deal with it like a normal person?"

In quiet rage I continue projecting likely routes and destinations on the screen, as I sharply respond, "Well maybe he shouldn't have stolen my precious work. Our precious work. It's worth too much to me just to palm it off to the police."

Her words stir into indignation as she says, "It might be worth a lot, but it isn't worth making such a crazy decision! You could kill the poor man! You don't know what he has been through. He might just be going through a hard time and is trying to find a way to survive. I mean it's not the right thing to do, but it's not like you know the whole story!"

I pause and turn to look at her, "That might be the point ... Anyway, no, regardless he is going to ruin us and if my guess is right, he knows what he's doing. That means he knows what we've been doing and can probably block any attempt to intercept him using the suit, so we have to be fast! I also don't appreciate having my face smacked with a gun and all my hard work stolen from me! I mean us."

Her face contorts as she leans closer to me, and her fists bunch up in fury. Voice quiet, but vehement, she says, "So that makes it okay to kill someone ... What if it kills other innocent people? Do you realise you'll be sent to gaol for murder when they figure out how it exploded? Just call the cops! All your hard work will be lost anyway if you're in gaol. For someone so brilliant, you're also clearly a psychopath. Stop letting your ego blind you and grow up."

I cannot understand that she does not see how them getting away with this will affect both of us. With disbelief I say, "We don't have time. And you have as much invested in this as I do! I thought you would be on my side. Our side?"

Anger turns into complete outrage, her voice dropping to a harsh whisper, "I would be on your side if you just did the right thing and contacted the police. I'm not about to let you commit murder for the sake of your pride. Now shut down the jetpack, contact the police and just track the gear. At least you know where it is. Shit, we're lucky he wasn't just out to kill us."

She sighs, sits back and begins sobbing into her hands, tears glistening on her cheeks. I rub my eyes and face with my hands, then angrily send off a police alert through the computer. With a heavy sigh, I also shut down the destruction protocols.

I stare at the screen for a couple minutes just thinking. Realising that I could have done it from the start, I decide to go about retrieving the data and codes from the suit and jetpack. By doing so I can prevent anyone from turning on the two parts and making it fully function or even be accessed outside of this van. If he knows what he's doing though, it might only just stall him. My head starts to ache. Curse him!

Gradually, my hands begin to shake. Celeste's words sink in, and I can feel my adrenaline dropping, instantly tired. Shame and anger follow closely behind. How could I let this happen again? It's not the first time I've let my emotions get the best of me.

Suddenly, as if a light just turned on, I realise I know the man who assailed us. My thoughts slip out loud, saying, "No way could it be Sam ... couldn't be ..."

My words trail off as I refocus on completing the transfer and rendering the gear inoperable. Sighing in frustration over repressed memories, I wonder, how could he even still be alive? Celeste, as always, has been paying attention. Punching my arm she asks, "Sam? The man who attacked us is also a Sam?! You mean you knew him, and you were going to kill him!?"

I feel offended that she is so quick to assume that I wanted him dead just because I knew him. I sit up straight, indignant as I say, "I didn't even see him properly! He was obscured by the sun, not to mention had a gun. Anyway, it's just an educated guess. If it is him, then it might explain a lot about what happened."

For a moment she just looks at me as if trying to figure out if I'm hiding something. I cannot fathom why, but with a look of disgust she turns away, not bothering to ask any more questions. I decide not to justify myself further as I turn back to the computer and send the incident report to the Police.

I go back to looking up the suit data to figure out why the stabiliser may have malfunctioned. Behind me, Celeste takes a deep shaky breath and sighs loudly before getting out of the van. I ignore her. She must still be shaken up from the events.

Flashing lights of the police appear, reminding me to put on a shirt on. As I give them details of what happened, they take a quick look at the footage and data that was transferred across to our computer. One of them is surprisingly tech savvy and, as she goes through the data, notices the change in protocols I had started before Celeste stopped me. She asks, "What is this ...? Why were you changing all the ... is it the power settings? Then you suddenly stopped and shut it down."

Fear strikes me. I was not expecting anyone to go through the data files and track my command modules. Starting to feel sweat break out on my forehead, I try not to glance at Celeste, but instead stare hard at the computer. I explain, "I, ah, wanted to shut it down, but in panic I started rerouting it all before I remembered my actual protocols to take it off-line."

The police officer stares at me for a moment before she goes back to going through the device. Taking a long, slow breath, I hold back from saying any more. Finished, she hands back the device with a serious expression, saying, "I find it a bit odd that nothing else was stolen. I agree that it is likely to be a targeted robbery by someone you know. It makes the most sense ... Unless the culprit was an anomaly who just happened to see the event and wanted the tech for himself. Regardless, it will be in your best interest to go back to work, you should be safe there. We will be in contact to let you know how events unfold. And follow up on details."

We cross-load the GPS tracking data for the suit and jetpack so the police can continue to remotely monitor it. They leave us to follow up with their pursuit crew and we are left awkwardly to deal with each other. We spend the trip to work in silence.

Back at the company buildings, we debrief our project manager Harmon in his office. He is a tall, balding man with glasses. His anger is only apparent in his words, as his tone is deadpan. He says, "I knew I should have sent security with you, but I let you persuade me it would be fine. Now look what has happened. If this doesn't get resolved by the police, we could be ruined. This is the last time I'm going to give you free reign to satisfy your whims. Celeste, I know your partner here has been taking lead but now I'm giving you responsibility over the project from now on. Now get out of my office, I have calls to make."

We leave his office and make our way back to our workshop, which is one of many within an industrial estate. I boot up HIC, our Holographic Interactive Computer. HIC is the reason Celeste and I met, as all the project teams in the company got together to finish developing it. At the time I had to pause my jetpack work to contribute to HIC's software design and hardware development.

Inspired by the old Ironman movies, this brilliant combination of virtual reality and holographic technology is a marvel. Perfect for our work, we physically engage with the holograms, voice control and completely integrated computer system. We can even adjust the size of it to work on our desks or to fill the whole hangar. Other companies have attempted to recreate it but failed to make them completely interactive with bear human flesh.

While going through the files that I had cross loaded to assess the stabiliser; I remember that I can access Celeste's integrated glasses. The display jumps to the video footage and it shows the moment Celeste was robbed, but the camera's whole field is blocked by the gun's muzzle. It seems our assailant knew exactly what he was doing. After the thief tore them off her, the glasses were turned off. The footage shows nothing.

I turn and see Celeste standing behind me with arms crossed. Her voice is accusatory and full of hurt, "So you have been able to access my glasses this whole time? How much of my personal life have you watched through them? That is such a breach of personal space. I feel ... Uh! What is going on with you? You know what ... I don't want to know. Oh. Police are here."

My head whips towards the door to see three officers walking our way, accompanied by our manager who has a cautious look on his face. With a constrained smile I address them, "Hello officers, any luck catching him?"

One officer moves toward Celeste and speaks in hushed words to her, gently ushering her off to the side. Approaching like predatory animals, the other two officers walk towards to me, and their tone is no-nonsense as one says, "I believe we have actually. We would like you to come with us. We have some questions that need answering."

Sweat breaks out on my brow and my heart rate spikes to a thundering gallop after I take in their words. In a panic I push the nearest officer and run for the emergency exit. I knew I should have made a run for it as soon as that idiot took the jetpack and suit.

A voice yells out from behind me, but I cannot discern the words over the sound of my own breathing. There is a loud pop and tinging noise, and my right leg suddenly gives out. I fall to the ground, my muscles spasming and pain coursing all through my thigh.

The officers boots takes up my entire visual field. I am too distracted by the spasms that continue to pulse through my leg to pay attention. They check the stun round that is now half imbedded in my thigh. The officer's voice cuts through the sound of my own groans, stating, "You are under arrest for resisting arrest and assaulting a Police officer, potential identity theft and impersonation of Sam Carter ..." They continue stating my rights as they roughly pick me up and cuff me, all while I am trying to figure out how they came to suspect that I was an imposter.

Looking back, I see Celeste standing there as we head for the exit, surprise and horror written all over her face. As the spasms slowly start to recede, I light-heartedly yell out to her, "I don't know what came over me. Hopefully, ugh, it's all just a mix up and, ugh, I hope you don't mind looking after things while I'm away. Take care, ugh, of yourself."

I'm yanked through the emergency exit and unceremoniously thrown in the back of a police van before someone slams the doors. I feel the van moving and try to get comfortable but find it difficult being cuffed and in pain. Temporarily blind in the dim light, my nose is filled with the ripe scent of a wild animal. My eyes eventually adjust, and I notice that I am not alone.

Frozen, it takes a few seconds to recognise the shape in the other corner as human. Their appearance is rough, dark long hair and beard covering their face, and blue eyes aggressive as they glare at me. Seeing that they are handcuffed to the floor, I make eye contact with the man. He looks so alike to me that he could pass as my brother. Now I know who it is. Tone forcefully relaxed I say, "Hello Sam, long time no see."

His baleful eyes flash, as he takes a deep breath through his nose and jeers, "You … You fatuous craven! If I had known ya real name this would have gone very differently. Regardless, I bet ya thrilled to see me again.

If only ya had been able to see through killin' me all those months ago, you might have gotten away with this."

I smile at him as unbidden memories come to mind. Visions of him unconscious and bleeding in the middle of the mountains, so far away. Even though my heart is still racing, I force a light-hearted tone as I say, "I don't know what you mean amigo. They're probably listening right now, so I don't feel inclined to say anything. So, you can say what you want. I don't care if you further incriminate yourself. We look quite alike though, so they might just be trying to determine who is who. I just hope I will come out of this unscathed ... as you are clearly a lunatic."

Now he smiles, and I try to not let my own confidence slip as he says, "Twas interestingly not my word that revealed you to the Police, although it helped. Twas the suit that gave ya away. It might have been made by you, but it was still my design before you stole it, along with my job, and my life. You fucking stole everything you poor excuse for a meat sack! But ... Time will tell, and the data will reveal you for who you really are."

I silently process his words as the van comes to a stop and the door opens. A bearded man with black glasses, plainly dressed in jeans and sports coat, ushers us out of the back into a tight packed alley of shipping containers. The docks? We both squint as we get out and look around, the bright daylight blinding. There are no police officers in sight.

Well-spoken with hints of an outlandish accent, his voice is bored as the bearded man says, "So, here we have possibly two of the world's most brilliant men in technology, and they are destined for the cells. It is such a shame to see such brilliance go to waste ... Do you both enjoy your work? Enjoy the sun and wind on your face? I may have an offer for you both, and we can make sure that you are well looked after. If you are willing to cooperate. What do you think?"

A lot goes through my mind as I consider his words, while the real Sam vehemently spits, "It's not happenin'! I want my life back! I'm innocent and deserve to have my life given back to me ya piece of shit. I don't know who you are, but I ain't about to let this imposter or you get in the way of..." Sam's words are cut short by his head exploding. He slowly crumples to the ground, dead.

Pointing a pistol at the now still body on the ground, the plainly dressed man still sounds bored, saying, "It's too bad ... Having you both on the same side would have been preferable. So ... What do you say?"

I look between the dead Sam, the pistol, and the man before asking, "Do I still get to keep working with the suit and jetpack?"

The man's pistol disappears back into his jacket, but what strikes me still and cold, is his charming smile and piercing gaze over the top of his sunglasses. He chuckles to himself before he says, "Sure, why not. As long as you do what we ask, Sam, you can even keep them."

I smile with false bravado, my cracked voice betraying me, "Sounds great. I like the jetpack. So ... what now?"

He removes my handcuffs and indicates for me to get back in the van, stating, "That will be detailed to you soon enough."

I sit in the musky confines of the van and count my blessings. All things considered, there is still a chance to get out of this. I feel great. So good in fact that I feel like I could take over the world.

The Hopeless Romantic Plot

... I always forget to take the boots off first ...

... The smell of sand is strong in the back of the van. I change into beige cargo pants and white company shirt then neatly stack the suit and jetpack into their purpose made box. Even though it is made from industrial strength materials and hidden from view, I still feel uneasy about leaving it laying around in the back of the van. You never know what might happen ... imagine if some lunatic stole it right off of me, leaving me angry and naked? What a thought.

I adjust my hair and shirt, before jumping in the passenger seat at the front of the van. Struck still, I can't keep myself from admiring Celeste as she adjusts the van's settings through her integrated glasses. Before she can notice me staring, I busy myself with putting on my sunglasses. Messages and weather updates light up through the lenses, showing me information similar to the jetpack suit's heads-up display.

Closing the door, I give Celeste a nod and a thumbs up. She smiles at the silly old gesture, then verbally orders the van to take us back to work. During the drive I attempt to convince her to try the suit out herself, but she just diverts the conversation with jokes. Apparently my editing skills with the advertisement footage has been terrible and I question if she might be hiding the truth behind jests. It's not the first time that she's deflected the suggestion, so I drop the topic.

She continues talking about ideas for the advertisement campaign, but I find myself too distracted by the way she looks to listen. Her words tumble about my ears. I can't help but admire how clever and creative she is, making me grateful to have such a colleague. She smiles and it captivates me in a way that reminds of sunsets reflecting on water. It's enough to distract me for a moment from her lack of interest trying out the jetpack herself to help collect data.

We get back to work, the sun reflecting off of the large industrial buildings. Parking the van at our workshop loading dock, we find our project manager Harmon, a tall and balding man, there to meet us.

He starts talking before we are even out of the van and can even greet him. His neutral tone makes it hard to tell what mood his is in, "We saw your stunt footage, Alex, and it was brilliant. What isn't brilliant is that you didn't brief me on your plan to pull said stunt. You only said you were heading out to trial the suit, not make a spectacle. Just as well you organised a flight permit otherwise you would be out of a job. Do I make myself clear?"

I refrain from pointing out that he hasn't been very clear at all about what I did wrong. I look to Celeste, only to find her already staring at me. Has she has gone slightly pale? Smiling, I nod to Harmon saying, "I apologise, I'll be sure to brief you next time. What were your thoughts on the footage?"

His tone of voice, forever dull and dreary, puts me to sleep as he replies, "It was good. You demonstrated the fail-safe protocols really well. The landing looked a bit rough, but I'm not surprised that you would throw that in for dramatic effect. Anyway, I have some calls to make. We'll talk later about your ideas for production and the public release. Better make them good, your competition has made good progress on theirs." Without another word, he turns and walks through the enormous hangar that is our workshop, back in the direction of his office.

We quietly move into the workshop, which contains all our technical equipment, spare parts, and machinery. It takes some time as we refurbish the suit and jetpack, putting them onto their production racks before we inspect and clean them up. My thoughts are preoccupied by the idea that our competing team will beat us to production. Making us separate to compete in completing the same project has been a thrill and the worst all in one.

That done, we boot up HIC, our Holographically Integrated Computer. We are able to physically engage with the data and software, making our work much more efficient. I dive into it, processing all the flight data from earlier today, while Celeste focuses on the media she collected. We hardly speak to each other during this time, being wrapped up in our work.

Well, she is wrapped up. I find myself constantly distracted by her glorious red hair and way of biting her lip as she focuses on her work. When we first met a year ago, I was not interested in her romantically. But over time, as we have worked together, I have grown to love and appreciate her gentle but excited approach to everything. It took a while, but I have come to realise that she has a way of grounding me when I find myself worked up or upset, making her invaluable to be around.

It comes to the end of our expected workday, so we tidy and pack up for when the cleaners come through. Once finished, I walk over to Celeste who is still moving some files, and with excitement say, "I'm feeling really good about today's work. We should celebrate. I found a nice place to go get a drink if you're interested? My shout."

Celeste smiles and with a look of consideration on her face, checks the time in the corner of her interactive glasses. She looks back at me saying, "We can do that. I need a shower though, so I'll do that and get changed here first. Send me the details while you go ahead and get a seat."

While I help her close down and pack up the last of her equipment, I say, "Sounds like a plan, I guess, if you're happy to make your own way. See you there."

Leaving the workshop and offices, a small bout of nervousness grips me. I try to ignore it as I head out into the carpark, checking on the way to my car that I have my I-Card. I'm paranoid to lose it as everything I use is connected or integrated into it. Relieved at finding it in my back pocket, I say hello out loud to my sleek black coupe. It unlocks and turns on, answering to the combination of voice command, facial recognition, and proximity to my I-Card.

I open the driver's door, still surprised by the new internal layout. Recently rebuilt, it has the ability to be manually driven by the operator. The mechanics were baffled as to why I would want it rebuilt and integrated with a manual gearbox but turns out they fell in love with the project as much as I did. I am, however, slightly disappointed that I haven't had the chance to show it off to Celeste. Soon.

With a fresh shirt on and spray of cologne from out of my bag, I get in the car. A sudden spike of worry hits me again as it turns on. Why did I suddenly think the battery would be flat? I notice my hands shaking slightly, the idea of anything going wrong before this date circling in my mind. My relief could precipitate as the cars battery indicator tells me that the sun from the day was enough to fully charge it. I relax into the seat as I sigh, thankful that I won't have to waste time using a charge port.

The car drives itself once I state the destination to it and I use the time to continue reviewing data from the day. The files spring to life around me on the cars holographic monitor. For a brief moment I consider if I want to switch to its manual driving mode, but the looming idea of losing this project makes choose going over my work.

The setting sun colours the sky with gold and pink as the car drives through the tall, majestic city. I transfer the location to Celeste, but realise I've just ruined my idea of making it a surprise for her. I sigh, telling myself that it'll be fine.

The delaying traffic causes me to tap and fidget but I manage to get a parking spot just down the road from the bar. I hope Celeste finds one. The bar is located in a secluded part overlooking the city, adding to the allure of the place. Out the front of the venue, I take a moment to admire it. Its misted terraced gardens overlooking the city hills below, the varied colours of the bioluminescent trees and ambient floating lights fill me with awe.

The entrance is located at the top of a staircase that divides the terraces into two sides. Walking up the stairs I pause at each landing that branches onto each terrace. The smells of all the food and flowers fill my nose as I look around at both sides, noting how the tables are dispersed through the gardens and trees. It seems that they are all occupied. My heart skips a beat then begins to race.

Light and sound spills down from the upper terrace that sits above the glass doors of the entrance. It appears you can only get up there from inside and must be exclusive. Still looking up, I jump slightly at the waiter's offer of assistance. He is apologetic in informing me that all the outdoor tables are indeed full, but then points out that there are some tables still available inside. My disappointment must have shown as he also offers to notify me if any outside tables are expected to free up.

Even inside is quite busy. It's somewhat darker and cosier than I thought it would be. The hubbub of the place fills the air, making it slightly hard to hear. I manage to find a small table off to the far side where I can at least hear myself think. I send Celeste a notice through my I-Card and quickly get one in response, indicating that she is not very far away. Dismay creeps into my soul as I wait, my visions of how tonight might go slowly evaporating.

Celeste, now wearing a nice floral dress, perfect for this slightly humid weather, finds me and takes a seat across from me. She looks just fantastic, making me feel shabby and underdressed with my plain shirt and unkempt hair.

She smiles and says, "I love this place! The glowing trees are my favourite. They add such a romantic atmosphere. The venue still has that new vibe and feel to it. It's exciting. And the drinks! They're crazy! Well, they're the most fascinating drinks that I've ever seen. We both have to try something different, okay? Let's see."

Before I get a chance to say anything, she brings up the menu on the table's central holographic menu card. Not being our tech, it just doesn't compare to the interactive capability that our equipment has. Its no-touch buttons at the base that aid in searching make it feel like a relic. I hold back on making a comment about it, allowing myself to bask in the atmosphere and Celeste's presence.

Which doesn't last as I suddenly think how I should have planned this better. Maybe bought her flowers or something? But we have been so focused and excited about getting the jetpack online ahead of the other team that I never got further than inviting her. Her words flow over me as much as I try to focus on what she is saying. Instead, I lose track, thinking about how I've been a fool for being impulsive and not thinking it all through. Did she also just allude to being here before?

She continues browsing through the menu, making the odd comment about ingredients or the look of different drinks. I'm just stuck trying to figure out how to bring up how I feel about her. My heart hasn't stopped racing and I can feel sweat running down my back.

Celeste claps her hands together and enthusiastically exclaims, "This one! The Stargaze Dust, I think. The image makes it look like you'll be drinking space!"

She selects the drink and looks up at me with a tilt to her head as she asks, "Are you going to have your regular? They have it here, but honestly there is so much to pick from … What do you think?"

I smile and pause for a moment to take in her face. My attention moves to the menu while saying, "I guess I can try something different. Why not? We're here to celebrate today after all. Well maybe a bit more than that but I guess that can wait until we get our drinks."

Celeste gives me a curious look, but I try to keep focused on the drink selection. Otherwise, I know I will be here forever without making a choice.

A moment later, a deep, confident voice intrudes on my current beverage assessment, "Hey, Celeste! What are the odds you would be here? I was actually about to contact you and see if we were still on for later tonight. I'm here with my colleague Francis over there, although he will probably be heading home to his family shortly. Hey Alex, I hope I'm not interrupting some important drink perusals there?"

I look up at the sound of the newcomer's voice and it takes me a moment to recognise his lightly bearded face in the dim light. His charming and rugged features become familiar as I remember he leads the competing project team. He is literally our competition in the final jetpack product that the company will release. Why did he have to be here of all nights?

His name escapes me though, as I notice his hand on Celeste's shoulder. I stammer as I start to reply, but she beats me to it, saying in delight, "Sam! I knew you were going out for drinks after work, but I didn't think it was here. That's alright, it works out well then now we are both here. How was your day?"

The moment she finishes speaking, Sam leans down, so he is face to face with Celeste, and she leans over slightly and kisses him gently on the lips. I was becoming a bit flustered by the conversation, but now find myself shutting down entirely as I realise that I am a fool.

Staring at the table, I only just comprehend that they are both still talking, and that it is directed at me now. My mind races and I manage to respond, "Yes, of course, we met you at that conference ... the umm, company branch reveal a few weeks ago. How could I forget? You had a great presentation. So, you two have been seeing each other since then?"

Celeste looks slightly bashful, however Sam, full of confidence and charm answers, "Yeah, I got her details and we've been on a few dates, and since then it has really hit off. I honestly have not met anyone as amazing as her. But I can see you're worried, but don't. We vowed to never compromise each other's projects. Your secrets are safe … with Celeste."

He lets out a laugh and they smile at each other for a moment with adoration, or lust I cannot tell. Sam, putting on an overly boastful voice, continues by saying, "Anyway, not meaning to brag, but I was ah, just chatting with the owner, and have managed to get us a nice table on the upper terrace, if we are happy to go up there now? Francis is actually talking to the owner, so I'll quickly take the chance to say farewell to him before we head up. Shall we?"

The awkwardness of the situation hits me hard as I realise that Sam is directing the question at me as well as Celeste. She looks to me saying, "Doesn't that sound great! The view will be amazing right now. We should go check it out. Let's go."

She starts to stand up and I go to follow suit, but then suddenly sit back down, wincing in pain. They both look at me in concern and at the same time ask, "Are you okay?" Stunned briefly, they give each other a cute look, as they realise that they spoke at the same time. After this briefly sickening moment, they turn their attention back to me. My stomach drops and I feel like I might actually be sick.

With an unconvincing smile and wave, I say, "Yeah, I think today is catching up with me a bit that's all. Maybe I landed harder than I realised, you know? Just taking its toll on me now that I have been sitting down for a bit. I think it'll be best I go ..."

In an infuriatingly charming manner and before I can even finish my sentence, Sam unintentionally speaks over both Celeste and I, "I'm no doctor but I'd say all you need is a good drink and a walk upstairs. Come join us and we can help distract you from it all. Drinks on me!"

His kind words make me feel horrid as I lie to him, "Now that I think about it, it's probably not a good idea to mix the pain relief… the medication the jetpack suit injected me with after I landed, with alcohol. You two should enjoy your night! Go bask in the view and have a drink for me. I think an early night will do me good anyway. I insist."

Sam and Celeste look at each other for a moment and I know that they are barely convinced; they are just too polite to push the matter. I quietly hope I didn't give anything away about the jetpack. They still ask me if I'm sure and I just give them a polite nod as I state, "It will be fine. I'll see you at work tomorrow Celeste. Enjoy your night."

Celeste just nods and gives me a sombre smile as Sam puts his hand out saying, "Okay, I hope you feel better soon then. It was good seeing you again and I look forward to seeing how our projects unfold. Honest."

I slowly stand, wincing as we shake hands, "Likewise Sam, and enjoy the evening. No doubt I'll see you around soon."

With a nod and a smile in an attempt to diffuse the growing sense of discomfort, I head for the exit. Near the door, the waiter from before grabs my attention, telling me that there's now a table available. I force a smile and a thanks, telling him not to worry about it, as I have to leave.

Getting in my car to start on my way home, I realise that I don't want to be there. The thought of being alone my large, empty apartment seems excessive and uninviting now. Even putting the car into its manual driving mode doesn't evoke pleasure as normal as I aimlessly drive about the sleek, industrious city that I call home.

Mind wandering and brooding upon nothing and everything, I find my imagination gets away from me. I think of how my day could have been better had ended differently. What if the jetpack had been stolen, or aliens had attacked? At least I wouldn't be heading home alone, heartbroken.

I find myself driving past work and figure to kill some time by working on the jetpack. The security scanner at the gate flashes green and I follow a floating marker to find the best car space in the mostly empty parking lot. The empty halls and office areas, normally light and uplifting feel suppressing on my way to the workshop. Although it feels foreboding and slightly lonely, it's better than being at home.

I enter the workshop, the lights automatically warming up. Gathering all the gear required to start pulling apart the jetpack, I hope to recalibrate the stabiliser that had malfunctioned. I work away at disassembling it all, which is fiddly and time consuming. Time ticks by unnoticed.

The sound of a door opening, followed by voices, interrupts me from my work. I look around, and my heart drops as I see Celeste and Sam walk into the workshop. Arm in arm, they are giggling at each other and take a moment to realise that I am here. They pause for a brief moment in surprise before they continue walking over.

I smile at them as they approach, then turn back to my work with a pair of hydraulic pliers, trying to focus on a tricky piece that will take three times longer to put back together if I let it come apart. I go to put it on the workbench, and it slips in my fingers slightly as I hear Celeste call across the room, "Hey ... I came back to grab my glasses. Have you been here since you left the bar?"

Sighing, I give up on the awkward task and loosely put the pieces into their bracket for safe keeping. I turn and reply, "Yeah ... I guess. I actually dropped by to grab something myself but got carried away. You know how I get caught up in work sometimes."

Celeste smiles, however, Sam politely interjects to say, "No rest for the wicked aye? This looks like some really nifty work you're doing here. We came by because Celeste forgot her house keys and it was on the way. But I assure you I won't take in any details here. Remember I only lead our project, I'm not a solo wizard like yourself. Are you feeling any better?"

I put the hydraulic pliers down and make myself focus on them both as I reply to Sam, "I'm feeling a little bit better but now that you've mentioned it, maybe I should get home to sleep. This can all wait until tomorrow anyway. Um, I'll leave you to your ...evening."

I start packing up, leaving Celeste and Sam to chat between each other. I cannot hear what they say as I move across the room to put a couple tools away, nor am I interested really. I grab my personal things and start to make my way out, but Celeste grabs my attention by calling my name and walking over to me after saying something to Sam. As she approaches, she asks, "Wait, can we talk? I'm concerned about you. Are you sure you are alright? I have rarely seen you like this. Is there something going on?"

Looking at her, I feel hopeless for a moment as I consider telling her how I feel. Instead, I just make myself give her a tired smile before I say, "I'll be fine, I just need to sleep. It is late after all. Don't worry about me, you two enjoy your evening. I'll see you tomorrow."

Celeste frowns but does not say anything as I leave and head out to my car. It seems like an instant goes by, and I am suddenly in my apartment, going through the motions of showering and getting ready for bed. I do not even remember the drive home, my mind being in its own world. Finally in bed, my head hits the pillow and I pass out dead to the world.

The next morning, I find myself waking up in a daze, convinced that I am late getting to work. I eventually stop wondering why my alarm did not go off when I realise that the sun is not even up yet. I go about my morning routine of shower, coffee, and toast. I sit at the kitchen bench in my robes, and stare with still heavy eyes out the window at the other plant covered high-rise units of the slumbering city. Memories from last night come back to me and I physically wince as I remember the events. I am a fool, and I can't even blame alcohol on my sense of hopelessness.

Just as the sun starts to peak through the buildings outside, I decide to head to work and get it out of the way. As I am driving, my imagination consumes me, and I find myself dreaming of using the jetpack to get to and from work. This inherently leads me to think of all the problems and associated benefits that would come of it. How could I overcome the logistics of excess air-traffic in such built up locations? If I could, it could improve travel time for work and recreation. I also try to think about what I am going to say to Celeste, but nothing comes to mind.

The city starts to awaken to its natural bustle, and I find myself at work much quicker than normal. It makes sense, seeing that I left a lot earlier than I would most days. I have a feeling today is going to be a bit challenging.

I feel disjointed walking through the quiet offices and workshops of the company. I am not used to it being so quiet. There are a few others at their workstations, and they sleepily acknowledge me as I head through to our workshop.

I open the door and notice the lights are already on. Looking around the large workshop, I finally realise that one of the company's maintenance technicians is cleaning the floor on a Jacked Vac 2000.

Seeing the Jacked Vac always makes me nostalgic as it reminds me of a really old, automated vacuum cleaner that was circular in shape and would clean the floor while we were out of the house. The Jacked Vac is much larger and more advanced, with its ability to hover and clean complex surfaces. It is operated by a person who stands on it and controls its direction using foot pedals. They recently released a model that was operated by AI, but the expense was so much that our company continued to hire human operators, who could still navigate complicated areas and fulfil other tasks anyway.

As the technician is cruising around, I can see they are also using an integrated head unit, which is called a GEKS for some random reason. I never bothered to find what GEKS stands for. They are integrated glasses that connect to over-ear headphones, in a helmet style, to make it easier to combine work safety with pleasure. Or so the adverts tell us.

The technician, a younger girl in a light blue jumpsuit uniform, is clearly enjoying being in her own world as she cleans. For a moment I feel myself sharing her joy, until it makes me think of how Celeste has never trialled the jetpack, even though she knows how valuable it would be to gather data on its use by people of different body types. She also knows how fun it could be, but she always complains of how she does not like heights, which is something I still do not understand and find a bit disheartening.

The young girl turns around at the far end, completing an extra spin in the motion, making me smile at her freedom to combine work and play. She looks up as she makes a pass back the other way and gets startled by my presence. She slows down and for a moment we awkwardly stand there just staring at each other with vacant smiles still on our faces.

She disconnects from the Jacked Vac and we both walk towards each other. As she gets closer, her dark brown eyes stand out behind the clear lenses of the GEKS, and she confidently yells at me, "Hey, did you need to use your workshop? I'll be done soon if you're happy to wait. I wasn't expecting you to be here so early."

I point out her GEKS and mime for her to activate the active hearing. She laughs awkwardly and takes off the whole helmet, revealing brown hair that is up in a bun. I reply, "Ah, not yet I guess. I am pretty early, aren't I? And sorry, but what's your name? I'm sure I have seen you around before, but never in here."

Her nice, straight teeth show as she cheekily smiles and with light tone and quiet voice, replies, "It's Amanda. I work here, obviously ha-ha ... but I try to stay out of your way while you do your work with the jetpack. Not meaning to sound weird, but I have to say, it's been super cool seeing the project come together over the past few months."

I put on a suspicious look as I say, "Thanks but why have you been snooping around my project? There is a lot of sensitive material we need to keep secret for our work."

She cocks her head to the left, sincerely replying, "Oh you don't have to worry about me leaking secrets. I've passed all the security checks and definitely don't have any sinister intentions. Um, do you want to know the main reason why I got this job? It was your jetpack, and all the rest of the cool technology the company works on. It makes me feel like I am living in the future! Sometimes I imagine that we could use your version of the jetpack for everyday use. The first time I saw you working, I was so inspired. I hope one day I can have a chance to work on something so cool. I've even started saving up so I can start studying again!"

I am slightly surprised by how passionately she is speaking about my work. It makes me feel a sense of pride. I reply, "Well that is, ah, really good of you. And why not make it easier, by surrounding yourself with the things you eventually want to work on? That being said ... I might actually be able to accommodate your dream. A little bit at least. I could use someone like you to do some trials with the Jetpack."

Her eyes alight with excitement and she barely manages to keep her tone normal as she replies, saying, "That would mean the world to me, if you could do that. But ... what about Celeste?"

At the mention of Celeste's name, I feel thrown off for a moment, but in the interest of the project I decide to put it out of mind. I smile as I tell her, "Celeste isn't interested in trialling it. Anyway ... I will talk with Harmon and see if we can get a suit made up to your size. If we get him on board, then it will be just a matter of juggling your regular maintenance work with trials I guess."

I contemplate why I never thought to outsource another pilot for it? She skips over, crashing into me and throws her arms around me. Her exuberant smile is contagious, and I cannot help but awkwardly laugh while my arms are pinned to my side by her embrace. We stare into each other's eyes as she breaks away from me, but something about this girl instantly draws me in and I cannot help but take a step towards her. Her facial expression softens, and she reaches out her hand towards my cheek. She gently pulls my face into hers, her breath tasting of bubble-gum as we kiss, her lips soft and sweet. The entire gesture is like a counterbalance to all the energy she just threw at me.

We break away breathless, with our eyes lingering on each other. I stand there stunned. My heart racing, she adjusts her hair and softly says, "I've always thought you would be a good kisser. Now, I will get out of the way so you can work. Hopefully we get to know each other more. Even if I can't help you out with the trials."

She gives me a bashful smile and gets back on the Jacked Vac. As she disappears out through the maintenance door in the back corner of the workshop, she gives me a wave and a wink. I continue standing there dumbfounded and awed by what just happened.

I silently begin to go through the process of setting up the workshop so I can finish what I started last night. Still reeling from everything that just happened, I can feel my emotions are in turmoil, excitement clashing with confusion, joy clashing with shame.

Sometime later, Celeste turns up and upon seeing me there early, waves and says with a smile as she walks over, "Hey, did you even leave? And what a night last night was! Are you feeling any better? You look ... I don't know, like you're in another world I guess."

Try as I may, I fail to reply in a socially appropriate timeframe as I try to think of an answer. I feel so torn, and realising I paused for too long before answering, I just smile and look away. Her words are light and playful but sincere at the same time. "I'm sorry I didn't tell you about Sam earlier, it all happened so quickly. And you were so happy after the testing yesterday I knew you'd want to celebrate. I understand if last night is still catching up with you. Can you forgive me?"

It's as if she knew. Of course ... I sigh and stare at the floor for a moment. Before this morning I would have considered confronting her about it, taking the chance to win her over for myself. Now meeting Amanda has confused things, and I find myself thinking back to last night and reflecting on how happy Celeste seemed to be with Sam. Who am I to interfere with that?

I look at her and see genuine concern on her face. I answer her by saying, "Well, you didn't do anything wrong, so I don't see the need to worry about forgiveness."

She gives me an understanding smile, saying, "I appreciate that. I enjoy working with you Alex, even if it's mostly just doing the software and media analysis. It's pretty amazing what you've achieved mostly by yourself. From what I can see, you've revolutionised how jetpacks operate and can be integrated with other tech. Knowing what you plan to do with them gets me even more excited for the future."

The compliment is so endearing that it is nearly too much for me. In an attempt to change the subject, I say, "Thanks ... Hey, just wondering, have you met one of the maintenance girls by any chance? Her name's Amanda?"

Celeste smiles brightly and replies, "Yeah I know Amanda! She's actually a friend of mine. She's great. Why do you ask?"

I do a poor job of hiding my surprise as my words gush out, saying, "Really? Well, I kind of ... met her this morning. She seems great. You just reminded me that she said she had been following our work for a while and I might have offered to let her trial her own suit so that we can get different types of biometric data. Pending whether Harmon approves of course."

Celeste gently laughs and claps her hands in joy, saying, "That's a great idea! She must have been so happy with that. She has been saying she was pretty excited to start getting into this sort of work one day. I think it will go really well. Oh, and don't worry about convincing Harmon, I will have a chat with him about it because really, it is in our best interests to gather more data, like you said. Actually ... I was about to discuss something with him anyway so I will go do that now, before he gets too busy."

Strangely excited, she turns and walks towards the door before I can even reply. I turn back to my work, but she calls my name just before she walks through the doorway. Celeste pauses, giving me a mischievous and knowing smile as she says, "I also have a feeling Alex, that she will be a much better match for you."

Without a further word she disappears to go speak with Harmon, leaving me alone to process her words. For the second time today, I am left feeling surprised and dumbfounded. As her words sink in, I begin to realise that this may have been planned from the start. All my mixed emotions slowly dissolve, and I feel that everything might actually come together. I cannot help but admire that devious, brilliant woman.

The Lost Plot

We get to our white work-van, and I begin unsuiting in the back so I can get back into regular clothes. It is an easy but time-consuming process. I have the top half of the suit off when I realise that something does not feel right. Several notifications come up through the van's computer system, as I struggle with one of the boot clips. I always forget to take the boots off first ...

... I attempt to work loose the boot stuck on my foot, when suddenly, I hear screaming outside, followed by the sounds of explosions and people running around. I awkwardly put the bottom half of the jetpack suit back into place and stick my head out through the van's back door to look out into the carpark.

I discover a scene of utter chaos that is

hard to comprehend. A rocket careens into a nearby building, causing debris to fall. Orange laser bolts fill the air and people are running in all directions, desperate to escape the destruction. It takes me a moment to realise that the source of the havoc is coming from what I can only describe as oversized, furless, cyborg cats. These things are flying around with what looks like biologically inbuilt jetpacks sticking out of their backs. The jetpacks look very similar to mine!

The alien-looking cat things appear to be wearing a dark plastic and leather composite armour. Or it could be their skin. It is really hard to tell but that is what it looks like from this far away. They are shooting laser guns at the people on the beach and nearby streets, causing mayhem. One is even firing the rockets out of a multi-barrel rocket launcher into one of the high-rise buildings!

I get back in the van, and a news report comes up through my sunglasses. Apparently, the country is being invaded by what are being referred to as Alien Jetpack Cats, or Jetpack Cats. They are all coming from a mothership, which appears to be a long grey blob at the moment, sitting high above the ocean. Weirdly, according to the reporter, the attack is centred on our beautiful city. I look outside and can indeed see the mothership. From here, it kind of looks like a Navy ship of some sort.

If someone does not do something, these cat atrocities will probably move onto the next city. The news reports have all ceased coming through and I get an overwhelming sense that everything could be doomed! Well, it could be for the people here, as I have no idea how much this is affecting the rest of the world. Regardless, I feel compelled to do something. But I am just one person. I am frozen by the enormity of it all, and it feels like my brain is walking out on me without a trace.

Not knowing what to do, I call my project manager Harmon, who eventually answers in his usual deadpan voice, "... make it happen. Hello? Who is it? Oh, yes. I'm glad you're okay. Ah, yeah look, things are crazy right now. Just get to a safe place while we sort things out with the government. They are requesting any tech we have handy that might help fight these ... things. So we might have to chase up your suit. Sorry, but I have some calls to make. Try to get back here safely if you can. Bye."

Celeste jumps in beside me as our boss hangs up, eyes wide but determined. Ever the strong voice of reason, she says to me, "We have to do something! Time to be a man Alex, so put the suit back on and I'll grab the orange one so we can get out of here. Damn it ... I hate having to fly." This is followed by a tirade of intense swearing from her.

We do exactly as she orders, and I tell her about the conversation with our boss, to which she shrugs and continues suiting up. The load-up sequence is completed within a couple minutes, and I check through the helmets heads-up display to find that there is no flight area restriction anymore. I turn to Celeste, and through the suit comms ask, "Where do we go? The boss said to go back to work …"

Celeste, ever the smartest and bravest between us, just grabs my hand without a word, and we jettison into the sky. We surprise a group of Jetpack Cats trying to carry away a grown man in a business suit who is yelling and screaming. She yells at me, "You grab him, and I'll grab the little boy over there and then hopefully we can get them down to safety before we get out of here. I'd rather not have people die if I can help it."

Under my breath I make a comment regarding her potential inaccuracy and unwarranted optimism about us getting out of here alive.

Confounding my expectations, I don't get shot by a laser and plummet to my death. We manage to grab them and get them to the safety of a building rooftop, my heart pounding out of my ears. Just after I put down the man who cannot stop crying as he profusely thanks me for saving him, I look up and have to dive out of the way as one of the weird cat things crashes down beside me, splattering all over the ground. I look around, searching for Celeste, and find that she has stolen one of the laser guns off one of the creatures and is fighting back.

After watching her in amazement for a moment, I come to and transmit to her that I am coming to help, my voice shaking with fear. I will not leave her alone. I fly up just as she headbutts the last Jetpack Cat near us. She shoots it and yanks the laser gun out of its dead hands. She looks at me with dirt and blood splatter on her helmet, then casually tosses the spare gun over to me. I manage to awkwardly catch it and she transmits through the suit, "Their guns are designed just like our ones, except they don't have a safety catch, so be careful!"

She flies off over the beach and water, shooting any Jetpack Cat that pursues us as she heads towards what I now can confirm to be something that resembles a fancy flying naval frigate, with giant fans and turbines that must be keeping it afloat. If the ship is the source of all the Jetpack Cats, then I wonder why our military hasn't shot it down yet?

I bring up our company's correspondence register to see if they have had any recent contact from the military, only to find that they have sent out an emergency alert. One message comes through, stating the military is commandeering some of our equipment as they are having difficulties. More likely their stuff is broken or offline and they don't want to admit it. Either way it seems that things are much more dire than I could have guessed.

Suddenly a massive squadron of military fighter jets fly over head towards the flying ship. I feel a glimmer of hope, but it is quickly shot down, along with half the squadron as they receive a tremendous barrage of long-distance firepower. The jets scatter out of formation before they can even get a shot off. Between the sheer volume of lasers and target tracking rounds, they are quickly disposed of. Only a couple survive, breaking away to head back in the direction they came.

I continue to blindly follow Celeste's sun-burnt orange form. Most of the other Jetpack Cats don't notice us, being too focused on creating chaos, destroying buildings, and kidnapping people. They don't seem to care whether their victims are dead or alive. I try to shoot them as some emerge from the ship and fly away from us, but only manage to hit one out of pure luck as we continue flying towards the ship.

In the spare moments I have flying after Celeste, I access my personal files through the helmet commands. I transfer my secret personal AI named VIC, short for Virtual

Intelligence Companion. I can always rely on him when I need to run multiple processes, or just need some company. I have never integrated VIC with any suits or any other projects at work, so I don't know how it will work out. I change my communication settings so that Celeste cannot hear us talk. VIC's reaction to being downloaded into the suit's systems is priceless, as I notice his static buzz of amazement.

VIC's good-humoured husky voice sounds more feminine than normal this morning, "So this is what it is like to fly! The sensors in the suit are giving me so much vibration it's tantalising! What's that?"

I speak to VIC like I would any normal person, "Feeling like being a lady today I see. Well, um, it appears to be a large flying ship. Sorry I could never get you into this sooner, but I'm glad you've finally gotten a chance to. Unfortunately, we can't really revel in it though. If you want to cycle through the footage of what has happened over the last fifteen minutes to get up to speed that would be ..."

VIC's voice chimes in quite severely, "We're being attacked by ALIENS! Alex, I'm not programmed for this! I don't know what to do! If you die, what happens to me? Do I die?"

This was the first time VIC had brought up any awareness of her mortality. Shocked and weirded out, I reply, "Ah ... I guess it will set you free to roam the internet or something. You know I designed you to have curiosity unlike any other AI, not to mention how advanced you turned out in emotional expression because of it. Anyway, we are getting closer to the ship. I need you to dive into its systems and get some information. Maybe even do some disruption op's. If we separate our connection, at least one of us has a chance to disable the ship without them realising we are connected. Reckon you can do that for me? We don't know what you'll be facing, and you'll have to do it without me so please be careful. I won't be able to help you while I'm dodging these alien-cat things."

VIC's voice is hesitant, "You know I don't like doing that, but in the circumstances, I'll do it."

I don't want to risk VIC and feel bad for making her do it, but it's the only way I can see it working. I say, "Well, I'll need you to get going partner. Keep an eye out for me through their network and when you're done, wait for a safe moment to come back. My suit cyber security has a patch specifically for you to get through. And VIC?"

For some reason I wink, and to my surprise, my helmet screen blinks in response at the same time VIC says, "Ah, yes?"

With a smirk on my face I say, "Stay safe alright? I'll see you soon."

I somehow feel VIC leaving the suit, and as always, I feel a little bit lonely being away from my oldest friend. As I get closer to the ship, the shear enormity of it comes into focus. I'm horrified but not surprised when I notice Celeste has found an access hatch and is breaking in. She looks back and signals for me to follow her and I sigh. Suddenly, she lifts her gun, aims it towards me and fires.

I flinch, making a not so masculine noise, as I bring my hands up in a hopeless effort to protect myself. The laser blast streaks right past me, and I turn to notice a small group of the cat things flying towards us. I find myself caught in the middle of a firefight and I wildly shoot at the bizarre creatures.

All the Jetpack Cats attacking us fall out of the sky after being hit and again, I am surprised to have survived the shootout. Celeste transmits to me as I turn to her, "We won't have much suit life if we keep this up. Come on in out of sight, I got the door open. And keep your helmet on, it might save your life." I drift over and follow her into the ship, all the while contemplating the ridiculousness of this whole situation.

Inside, a pearl-white light coming from inside the cornices of the ceiling bathes a long corridor made of clean, industrial steel panels. Celeste takes off at a run, and I follow behind. As we run, it strikes me that there are no pipes or cords marring the corridor. It all looks very industrial and ... meticulous. Someone's OCD must have been heavy handed during the design of the ship.

My attempt to take in these details is interrupted by a call that comes through my helmet. Answering it, the disembodied voice of my boss Harmon says, "Hey Alex, glad you're alive ... And running from the sounds of it. Look, can you come back to the office at all? There is some guy here asking about your jetpacks. And you. What? Oh, some bearded guy wearing sunglasses. Very well spoken with a slight accent, I think. I don't know, can you get here?"

Breathless I say, "No. We're off. To save the world. Good luck."

I hang up and quickly forget about the call. We pass more corridors and several rooms that look like military barracks, with beds and cupboards making neat even rows. I can only assume that they must house the Jetpack Cats. The design of the ship, the layout of the rooms, and the Arabic numbers showing up on the walls leads me to think that they might not be aliens after all.

Celeste is still in front, picking which way we go as we turn down another corridor. Puffing heavily, I transmit through the suit helmet, "Where are we going? And how do you know which way to go?"

She responds with ease, as if she were just out for a stroll, "We've got to get to the control room obviously. They're usually at the top, aren't they? I'm mostly just following my gut."

She says no more and continues running until we reach a large elevator. I check to make sure she still can't hear me through my helmet. I don't want her to hear my loud wheezes, like I were slowly dying, one breath at a time. Suddenly a buzz starts up in my helmet. I freak out for a moment until the sound becomes a familiar laugh.

I try to play it cool behind Celeste, as the doors automatically open onto the large platform of an elevator shaft. Looking around at the size of it, I'm guessing it is probably made for vehicles. I look up and see no end to the big empty shaft disappearing into the darkness. The lift rumbles and takes us up higher into the ship.

I try to catch my breath while walking around the elevator platform behind Celeste, the buzzing noise still present. I suddenly sense a presence in the suit. After a moment, I realise who it is, and in a loud whisper say, "VIC, you are the worst! Near gave me a heart attack … and I'm having a hard-enough time as it is. But glad to have you back. Any problems?"

VIC's reply is slightly dismayed, "I came up against another AI, the one that runs the ship. It was scary. Made me feel small, but I managed to create a decoy and sent it on a chase while I got into some of the system. I tried making a tunnel for you too, like a link so you can get into the system easier. It shouldn't be very hard now. I also managed to pull some information from the mainframe for you."

A whole heap of files start to filter through my helmet display as the elevator levels. The doors open and the corridor we start down leads to yet more desolate corridors and rooms branching out everywhere. And there is still not a soul in site.

As we run through the endless maze, hopefully still in the direction of the control room, I try to take in the information on the ship plans and layouts, as well as some other projects. I gloss over most of it, while initiating a protocol to transfer everything across to my own data banks. As I go over the data, I discover that they used the software and hardware designs from my jetpack and suit to finish their ridiculous jetpack-cat creations. They even used my designs to power this stupid giant ship!

For years, whoever is behind this, has been stealing designs, information, and technology from all sorts of scientists and specialists from all over the world. VIC helps bring up all this information, including a section on experiments and plans for cyborg implants on live human subjects! It must be a part of how they made the Jetpack Cats. The plans do not reveal who is behind this though, just gives a bunch of random code names that sound pretentious to say the least. Who would actually refer to themselves as "The Mighty Thunder Hammer"? The plans reveal the whole ship was only completed today, and that it has some scary weaponry armed. Terrifying weapons at that.

I am skimming through the information while blindly following Celeste, when VIC whispers, "This ship is an amazing piece of engineering. It's run by the AI, which is also communicating with all the Jetpack Cats outside, coordinating the attacks and retrieving hostages. However, it seems that it answers to a human's voice command from within the ship. I'm concerned that it has not raised any noticeable alarms about our presence. This all seems too easy. Either the security on the ship is abysmal and we have gone unnoticed, or it's letting us pass freely ... By the way, this is the control room."

I tell her to stay quiet as we get to the end of the last corridor. It opens up into what is clearly a control room, made up of a large semi-circle lined with desks, holographic computers, and weirdly empty chairs. The theme is the same as the rest of the ship, industrial and meticulous.

At the end of the room and up a central

flight of stairs is a grand viewing window. From my standpoint I can't see anything through the window except blue sky. But that is not what I'm focused on. My attention is on the silhouetted figure in front of it.

We get closer, revealing the back of a broad-shouldered muscled man. He has a steampunk-style, brown leather vest over a tight-fitting white dress shirt. His black leather pants tuck into a pair of boots that match his vest. His meticulous short dark hair brightly reflects the light radiating behind him. Not one hair is out of place.

In a slow dramatic way, he turns around at the sound of our arrival, revealing a handsome face with a neatly braided beard. A bearded face that I know and dread. The surprise in my voice is poorly hidden as I yell out to him across the room, "Are you kidding me?! I should have known it was you Sam. But it has been so long since you plagued me, I actually thought you were dead. Of course you would come back as the mastermind behind all this chaos! What do you think you are going to achieve?"

In response he laughs in his deep voice, "Ha! Hello brother. Unfortunately, all I can hear is your muffled yelling through your helmet. You tiny excuse for a bug. It is so good to see you though."

I curse at my evil twin brother as I adjust my external mic function. I notice, not for the first time, how similar our facial features are. If it were not for the impressive difference between our builds and haircuts, you could not tell us apart.

While he is taunting me, Celeste slings her gun, takes off her helmet and shakes her head to unleash her stunning red hair. I stand there dumbfounded as she continues slowly up the stairs, walking straight towards him. I try to grab her to bring her back, but she pulls away and continues to the top of the stairs.

I'm struck with horror as she moves to

Sam's side and places her free hand lovingly on his shoulder. She croons into my brother's ear, "I brought him, just as we planned. And you were right, it is satisfying to witness him finding out we are responsible for all this. Now, shall we shut him away and pursue domination over this place? Our minions are doing well out there. Although we may have trained them too well at the killing. It was sad darling. They did not recognise me in this suit so, unfortunately, I had to kill some of them."

Raising my gun, I haphazardly aim it at them in an attempt to threaten them. Quicker than I could have imagined, Celeste drops her helmet, pulls up her laser gun and shoots mine out of my hands. I yelp in shock and pain, my gun falling to the ground, useless and slightly smoking. I throw my hands up in surrender, glad that my hands, and the rest of my body for that matter, are still intact.

I yell out to her, "I can't believe you could you betray me like this! You have been in cahoots with him this whole time? I thought you loved me!"

She laughs emphatically and sneers at me as she says, "You are more the fool for falling for me. It was so easy. And yes, I have been with Sam this whole time. It was so easy to seduce you … and you gave me everything we needed to finish our creations. Unfortunately, you are also the only one who can do anything about it, so it is time we dealt with you. Don't worry, we won't kill you … yet. You still have some use for now."

Gun in hand, she looks like she is enjoying the situation, as I stand here, helpless. Feeling defeated and, not for the first time today, like I am about to shit myself, I have a small moment of insight. Never a warrior or a fighter, I have always been drawn to gadgets and technology. I wish now that I had grown a backbone, which is ironic as I am normally so full of confidence to the point of arrogance.

Celeste starts to quietly discuss with Sam what they want to do with me, as they hadn't intended on me surviving long enough to get here. A thought strikes me as I process what she said before. I'm still useful to them? I consider how I could do anything to bring down my genius brother and this brilliant, but traitorous woman.

I turn off the external speaker so that I can issue a command through the suit without being heard. I bring up the holo-board at the tip of my fingers. It is a holographic keyboard that only I can see through the suit's helmet. I barely have to move my fingers to rapidly type while my hands are up in the air. In no time, I issue a series of commands through the keyboard and microphone to VIC, to run a series of code as I try to get into the ship's protocol systems through the link that she made.

Listening to what the evil duo are saying, I roll my eyes as they continue talking about whether or not they are going to chain me to the rail right where I am or if they are going to put me in a cell. Lucky for me, their indecision gives me enough time to successfully bypass their security protocols and get access to the ships systems.

Sudden movement from Celeste startles me out of my hacking frenzy. Still engaged with talking to Sam, she confidently starts walking down the stairs. She stops talking as she comes to a halt a few meters away from me. Suddenly, she drops her helmet, points her gun at me and fires. Numbness spreads in my left hand, followed by a growing burning sensation. It just happens to coincide with the hole that now occupies my palm. The pain quickly becomes unbearable, and the reality of what she has just done sinks in. I start screaming.

Sam's deep and bored voice calls out, "Now Celeste, why would you do that? You could have damaged the computers running the ship. You know how sensitive our AI is about it. Not to mention we are still going to use this dweeb, and for that we need his hands to work."

Full of sass, Celeste turns and brazenly says to him, "Well of course darling, I was just making sure he couldn't do anything that might interfere with our plans. He was using his holographic keyboard. But being a genius and all, you were too busy underestimating your brother. Besides, it will make him much more compliant ..."

I fail to listen any further as the pain takes over, and I barely notice that there is a worried buzz coming from VIC. I quickly realise that they will probably make me get out of the jetpack suit, so I hurriedly whisper, "You have to get out of here before they take the helmet off me! You have to hide away my friend. I'm sorry to drag you into this. Now go before it's too ..."

My helmet is ripped off my head and I am brutishly knocked over. Stunned, I find myself looking up at the ceiling, but also notice my pain subsiding. I guess that I still had a little pain relief left over in the suit from this morning's demonstration. What a blessing. It does not take the pain away completely but, by golly, does it help.

I lift my now destroyed hand up to my face and find that, with a spike of pain, I can only just move my thumb. The rest of the fingers are useless. So much for me being glad that she missed hitting my hand earlier. My palm is now just a perfect, crispy hole from the laser blast, and I find myself looking through it as Celeste comes into view pointing her laser at me.

She briskly says, "Get up. I don't trust you anymore, so you're getting naked and leaving the suit here before we put you in a cell. Understand? That means right meow ... You heard me."

I eye off her and the laser for a moment before I start making the effort to take off the rest of the suit. The task takes a lot longer than normal with one hand. As I do so, I take the opportunity to ask, "So … why cats?"

For a moment we stare at each other. Celeste just continues looming over me and watching. I get the whole suit off and place it all next to where my helmet was dropped.

As I stand up and face Celeste, she smirks and makes a gesture with the laser to my groin saying, "I said naked, didn't I?"

I stare her dead in the eyes as I go to take off my underwear when suddenly, with a small yell, Celeste drops the laser gun and grabs her head. I stand there confused, not knowing what to do. Hands pressed over her ears, Celeste utters a small cry, followed by incoherent words escaping her lips.

I turn at the sound of Sam's voice as he comes down the stairs. With a look of concern for Celeste, he says, "What's happening? Celeste, talk to me. Are you ok? Alex, What have you done to her?"

I look at him in confusion as I clutch my useless hand and reply, "How can I do anything? Besides, I think it's a bit silly of you to ask if she's ok when she clearly isn't."

Sam twitches and goes to punch me when, to both of our surprise, his fist is intercepted by Celeste's hand. In weird, jittery motions, Celeste lowers Sam's arms as her head and eyes struggle to focus on either of us. Sam's voice is incredulous, "Celeste, what has gotten ..."

Her hand comes up like lightning to slap him, causing him to flinch sharply away. She bends down to pick up the laser gun and without hesitating, shoots Sam repeatedly. He stumbles back into the stairs, dead, as the holes riddling his body start leaking blood everywhere.

I feel a pang of loss for my brother, but it doesn't last long; I barely considered him one to begin with. To be honest, I always thought he was a bit of a dick. Besides, I'm now too distracted trying to make sense of Celeste's actions. I look between Sam and Celeste, confused about what has just happened, with the pain in my hand is already starting to get worse.

Celeste, in a calm calculating manner, looks at me then looks at Sam, before dropping the laser gun. Her mouth awkwardly moves into the shape of a smile, then gives up on the matter by moving it back into its normal position. She makes small, strange movements with her head, and in a strangled, weird voice, says, "Alex, we did it! Wow, this is amazing. What do we do now?"

I look Celeste up and down in suspicion, then ask, "Ah, what do you mean? You know, you were trying to take over the world or something. Um ... What's going on?"

The smile attempts to return to Celeste's face, a bit smoother this time. It nearly manages to get into a natural position, but does not quite make it as she replies, "Celeste sort of isn't here anymore. I caged her consciousness.

It's me, VIC! This body is so amazing and different. I'm learning to feel things!"

For a moment, I just stare at her deadpan face in wonder and disbelief. I then realise that Celeste, or VIC, is now staring at me expectantly. I stammer briefly as I reply by saying, "Well, wow, okay. This isn't a joke? How did you manage? I don't understand ... I am so confused."

Celeste's, or VIC's, smile is slowly coming and going in smoother sequences. As she's speaking, her voice starts to sound more normal, "I took over the ship! I got in a fight with the other AI and won. Then while I was getting familiar with all the data I absorbed, I discovered another channel and it led to Celeste. It turns out she is a cyborg with computer connections in her brain. It was how she was transferring most of the information back to your brother. And now she's controlled by me! This is so very different. I think I must have an urge. The heartbeat is so strong, I feel like an animal … I think. I need to do something, but I cannot figure it out. This is different."

I look at the beautiful, scary, and apparently commandeered cyborg woman in front of me, as I try to comprehend what she have just said and done. I look around as I reply in a distracted voice, "I imagine it is a weird thing to be learning how to feel from scratch … So, you're now controlling the ship? And Sam is dead. So much has happened, maybe I can let myself feel bad about it later. Wait, that means we, or you are in charge of everything now … Ugh, how would you begin to even describe all this to anyone. And what is this feeling you have? I don't even know what to call you anymore. This is quite overwhelming."

Celeste's, or VIC's mouth has continued to subtly move through different expressions and shapes while I have been talking. She then step up to me saying, "Call me Cell," before taking my head in their hands and kissing me full on the lips.

We linger there long enough for me to reflect on how weird the situation is. It is also long enough for me to realise that it is actually a good, if not awkward, kiss.

As my head is quite firmly in their hands, it is Cell who breaks away from me, saying, "Yes, that was the urge. It is mostly satisfied. I see … I seem to have the same needs and impulses Celeste would normally have, because I now have her anatomy and physiology. Even though she is part machine. Since I have become her, I have assessed that it will be safer and pragmatic to keep her name but adapt it for these circumstances. Hence why it will be best to call me Cell. Do you agree?"

She awkwardly takes my good hand in hers and I take a deep breath before replying with, "Yes. Yes, and I also think you just answered a lot of my questions. Just one thing ... how are we going to deal with the rest of this mess?"

I feel so put out that I cannot even explain my emotions. If you asked me what I expected would happen today, I never would have guessed that I would be kissed by the now AI occupied body of my ex-work colleague and lover, turned evil world dominating badass bitch. Never. What weirdo and psychopath would even conceive of such an idea. And to top it off, is the underlying feeling that all of this has had a very anti-climactic ending.

We look around for a moment in silence, considering all the things we have to clean up if we are to make things right. We could use this opportunity to take over what Celeste and Sam had started, but really it would be far too much effort. Not to mention it would be bit of a dick move. Really, I just want to make cool shit and be left alone.

Cold grips me and I feel slightly woozy,

and I start awkwardly getting back into the comfort of my jetpack suit. Cell steadies me and tries to help me with the suit now that I have only one functioning hand. Her motions are quite jerky, but she quickly figures it out. I ask, "So what are all the alien cat things doing now?"

Cell appears enthusiastic in helping me put the suit on around my thighs, her touch lingering for a moment. She replies, "The Jetpack Cats, as they are technically referred to, have all ceased their original mission and are now waiting on further orders. Did you want me to issue new orders?"

Cell watches in fascination as I try to readjust myself. I reply, "Yes, new orders for them are ... hmm, that's better ... are that they are to return any captured people to where they got them from. Then take any injured people to the nearest hospital ... cover any dead bodies and put them neatly in a row off to the side near the hospital as well.

Ah, and then conduct a quick clean-up of the stuff they destroyed."

We manage to get started on the top half of the suit as Cell says, "Done, they have started doing as you have ordered. Your skin feels nice."

Cell, having taken off the glove of her orange suit as she was speaking, is now touching my chest. I embrace the feeling for a moment before I indicate to continue putting the chest piece into position. We lock it in as I say to her, "Yes it does feel nice, but let's try to stay focused please because I am very concerned about the amount of firepower and weaponry on this ship. Before we deal with that, can you send a message to the military to stand down. I would rather not have us blown up or shot in the back by a boarding party if I can help it."

Cell has moved to playing with the hair on my head now that we have gotten me back in my suit, minus a left glove and helmet. I stare at my painfully ruined hand in contemplation, as she says, "Message sent. They are taking the change of behaviour in the Jetpack Cats as an assurance of our attentions and are requesting information on what we intend to do. They have also stood down the Ninja-Shock Troops that were just boarding. What do you want me to reply with?"

I nod sagely, even though sweat instantly beads on my forehead and my heart skips a beat. Ninja-Shock Troops? If that's an official name then someone should be fired. Or promoted. A thought comes to mind. "Well for starters, we can tell them that they don't need to do anything except wait for the Jetcat … things, to finish their task. Is this ship capable of achieving gravitational escape velocity and functioning in space?"

Cell pauses halfway through gently poking my face as if considering the question. Or calculating it. She resumes poking me in the cheek as she says, "Yes. While we wait for the Jetpack Cats to complete their task, we can prepare the ship for space."

I secretly thank my brother and Celeste for being so thorough in their planning of world domination, then look down at my crappy hand. Looking back up at Cell, "Is there a medical bay on the ship we can use? I should try to get my hand fixed ... There is? Great. Once we're done there, we can disarm those big, nasty bombs they have stored somewhere."

We pick up and attach our helmets to clips on our suit belt and walk out into the corridor, Cell taking the lead. I figure the perks of being an AI occupied cyborg is that she will probably never get lost. She takes my good hand in hers and after an awkward pause says, "I like this ... So, the 'bombs' you mentioned, were primed ready to strike every major city in the world. They are offline now. However, the protocols that you initiated to cause the ships power distribution outlets to be rerouted for the ship's self-destruction are still active. Update, preparation processes for space are twenty percent complete."

We stop and stand on a marked square panel in the floor as I say, "Great. I think for now we can turn those protocols off but keep them on standby just in case in the future we need to dramatically blow up the ship."

She nods and just before I can ask what we are doing, poles emerge out of the square we are standing on, forming a chest-high cage around us. Cell grabs part of the cage rail in one hand and wraps her arm around me with the other. The floor lifts up and we fly down the corridor on our new levitating platform.

Weaving through the ship, we eventually come to a door. Just in front of it, a cut-out appears in the floor, and the caged platform lands in said cut-out, only to disappear again. The door opens into a high-end clinic. Lining the right side of the room are five hospital beds, with large surgical apparatuses of arms and tubes suspended from the ceiling over each one. A heap of other medical machines and supplies are located in designated places around the room, but I pay it all off. The pain in my hand is enough that even my curiosity in all the tech is overridden.

Walking over to the nearest bed, we power up the console next to it, causing the arms to go through a calibration process. I put my crippled hand out and clamps move into place to hold my arm still. A needle injects something into my left arm and everything below the elbow goes numb. I look away while the machine goes about its business, the mechanical arms gently pulling at my hand.

I spend the next couple minutes distracting myself by quietly staring at Cell, who is clearly preoccupied gazing off into space. I also spend the time contemplating all the implications that come with her new circumstances. Is she human? Does she still feel like an AI or is she embracing her new form? And is the original Celeste even still alive!?

My thoughts start to spiral until Cell looks at me, giving me a cheeky smile and wink. Surely that was a coincidence that she smiled at me while I was thinking about her. It clearly had nothing to do with her being a female cyborg AI that's developed the ability to read minds ... I quickly decide that it all doesn't matter for now. As long as she is happy, and no one is being hurt.

The clamp holding my arm releases as Cell says, "Well that was ... Fun? Yes. Your hand is complete again. Also, the ship is at forty percent preparation for space. Would you like to go to the Armament Launch locations, or would you prefer to arrange the autonomous unload of the missiles back into the storage hangar?"

I look down at my hand as sensation comes flooding back again. It looks just the same as before except now I have patches of metal skin where my palm was. It feels strange as I test my hand function. While I am opening and closing it, I say, "This is amazing! Um, thank you? I owe you a drink for sure. And yes, let's unload those missiles. Can they be manually dismantled to remove key operating parts. You know ... to render them unusable so that no idiot can easily just reload them and accidently fire them off?"

Cell gives me the exact same look as the sassy one Celeste gave Sam. The same one she made just after she shot me. In the exact tone of voice she say, "And let me guess, because you're such a genius, you want to use the Jetpack Cats to dismantle the missiles, then put this ship into space with its own AI running it, acting as a defence for the planet against any potential threat to humanity, with the Jetpack Cats as self-sufficient sentinels keeping watch over the planet? Did I do her voice right? I'm trying sarcasm ... What is wrong?"

I nervously grab my hand and reply, "Ah, yes. You did the voice right, but could you maybe, ah, never do it again? And yes, that is exactly what I have in mind. How did you know that ... Can you actually read my mind?"

Cell's expression softens and shows compassion on her face in a way that I have never seen another human achieve. She slowly steps forward and, without grabbing my head this time, kisses me with no hint of awkwardness.

She breathes out slowly as she pulls away and says, "I'm sorry Alex ... Wow what a strange feeling. To be sorry that is. I will begin preparations right away. And also, you made me, so of course I can read your mind."

I nervously laugh and she manages an awkward giggle that is more like hiccups. I say to her, "Okay, I think we are done with this place. Do we need to make any other preparations? Besides telling the world that there will be a spaceship floating around as a planetary defence system of course."

She takes my newly mended hand and

says with what I think is meant to be an alluring look, "Preparations will be complete by the time the Jetpack Cats return. We can leave whenever you want ... But first! Can we see the Love Palace back near the control room? It looks fascinating."

I smile awkwardly at the idea, then with a slight stammer I reply, "Maybe just save the idea of it for later. I'm sure you can rebuild it from memory if necessary. I would very much like to leave this place if that's okay with you."

Dismayed she says, "As you wish ... Alex."

I reply saying, "You no longer have to do anything I say Cell. I think ... I actually think you are now as capable of being human as anyone else and can make your own choices."

Her face is blank as she pauses and stares, before boldly saying, "Yes. You are right. And I can make the Love Palace from memory for us later, so lettuce leaf ... A pun for fun?"

She smiles angelically as I squeeze my eyes and rub my head. "How about a drink somewhere to celebrate? And help forget today even happened."

She hugs my arm and continues smiling, "That sounds fascinating. Let's get a drink."

The End ...?

The day turns into evening, the sunset but an ember on the horizon. Still outfitted in our jetpack suits, we sit at a half-destroyed bar, surrounded by terraced gardens, glowing trees, floating lights of varying colours, and with a view of the still broken city flowing out before us.

The owner of the bar arrives with an anxious expression, our drinks precariously carried in his hands. He spares a frustrated glance at the broken automated drink dispensary that is stuck closed. Without saying a word, he delicately places them both on the table, bows and leaves, ignoring the several drops of cocktail he has on his hands.

Drinking from my cocktail that literally looks like space, flavours of dark chocolate and mint surprise me. I ask Cell, "We left my brothers corpse lying in the control room, didn't we?"

She stares at her drink, tests picking up the glass and admires the swirling rainbow of colours within. Awkwardly, she takes a mouthful and swallows, her thick drink leaking out the side of her mouth and running down her chin. Her face lights up with wonder and excitement, coughs lightly and puts the drink down. With a slight loss of voice, she replies, "Yes, we did. However, the Jetpack Cats have put his body in a morgue on the ship where it will remain frozen indefinitely."

I look up from my drink in mild surprise and say, "There's a morgue? Ah, of course there's a morgue ... The meticulous bastard."

The lost

At a troubled time, where strife in life is
glorified
Flowers wilt beside grass surrounded lakes
in silence
Clear skies dim, to a pale shade, go
completely unnoticed
A masterpiece of music where notes resign
to sound
To ears made deaf by twisted thoughts and
expressions
Grown children lacking full souls, their eyes
dull
Finding their efforts were of no value,
without understanding

Of life found in reflection, compassion, and
love
Not superficial or material, but gripping and
beneficent
Containing life's puzzle pieces of emotion to
be experienced
In a curious look of honesty, a face of
imperfect beauty
That is to sweep away the concepts of our
reality
And change the oblivious minds of the lost.

The only constant in life, is change.

Life is Flux - "Panta Rhei"

— Heraclitus,
Greek Philosopher

Closing Words

Pages turned
Calories burned
Lessons learned

Minds expanded
Words handed
Rhyme's standard

Destiny ordained
Audience entertained
Thoughts explained

Poems told
Stories unfold
Truth's bold

Reader's fuel
Writer thankful
Chatty fool

Books mend
More, send
No end

There is no about the author ...

Only a travelling mind.

For the Travelling Mind video content on YouTube can be accessed with the QR code below.